The River of Stars

Edgar Wallace

2015 by McAllister Editions (MCALLISTEREDITIONS@GMAIL.COM). This book is a classic, and a product of its time. It does not reflect the same views on race, gender, sexuality, ethnicity, and interpersonal relations as it would if it was written today.

CONTENTS

The River of Stars 1
Edgar Wallace 1
THE PROLOGUE 1
I. — AMBER 8
II. — AT THE WHISTLERS 15
III. — INTRODUCES PETER, THE ROMANCIST 23
IV. — LAMBAIRE NEEDS A CHART 33
V. — AMBER ADMITS HIS GUILT 47
VI. — IN FLAIR COURT 54
VII. — AMBER GOES TO SCOTLAND YARD 61
VIII. — FRANCIS SUTTON ASKS A QUESTION 70
IX. — AMBER SEES THE MAP 76
X. — THE MAN IN CONVICT'S CLOTHES 85
XI. — INTRODUCES CAPTAIN AMBROSE GREY 94
XII. — AMBER SAILS 105
XIII. — IN THE FOREST 113
XIV. — A HANDFUL O' PEBBLE 123
XV. — IN THE BED OF THE RIVER 132
XVI. — AMBER ON PROSPECTUSES 140
XVII. — WHITEY HAS A PLAN 150
XVIII. — WHITEY'S WAY 159
XIX. — AMBER RUNS AWAY 173
XX. — CHAPTER THE LAST 183

THE PROLOGUE

THE road from Alebi is a bush road. It is a track scarcely discernible, that winds through forest and swamp, across stretches of jungle land, over thickly vegetated hills.

No tributary of the great river runs to the Alebi country, where, so people say, wild and unknown tribes dwell; where strange magic is practiced, and curious rites observed.

Here, too, is the River of Stars.

Once there went up into these bad lands an expedition under a white man. He brought with him carriers, and heavy loads of provisions and landed from a coast steamer one morning in October. There were four white men, one being in supreme authority; a pleasant man of middle age, tall, broad, and smiling.

There was one who made no secret of the fact that he did not intend accompanying the expedition.

He also was a tall man, heavier of build, plump of face, and he spent the days of waiting, whilst the caravan was being got ready, in smoking long cigars and cursing the climate.

A few days before the expedition marched he took the leader aside.

"Now, Sutton," he said, "this affair has cost me a lot of money, and I don't want to lose it through any folly of yours—I am a straight-speaking man, so don't lose your temper. If you locate this mine, you're to bring back samples, but most of all are you to take the exact bearings of the place. Exactly where the River is, I don't know. You've got the pencil plan that the Portuguese gave us—"

The other man interrupted him with a nervous little laugh.

"It is not in Portuguese territory, of course," he said.

"For Heaven sake, Sutton," implored the big man in a tone of exasperation, "get that Portuguese maggot out o' your brain—I've told you twenty times there is no question of Portuguese territory. The River runs through British soil—"

"Only, you know, that the Colonial Office—"

"I know all about the Colonial Office," interrupted the man roughly, "it's forbidden, I know, and it's a bad place to get to, anyhow—here "— he drew from his pocket a flat round case, and opened it—" use this compass the moment you strike the first range of hills—have you got any other compasses?"

"I have got two," said the other wonderingly.

"Let me have 'em."

"But—"

"Get 'em, my dear chap," said the stout man testily; and the leader, with a good-humoured shrug of his shoulders, left him, to return in a few minutes with the two instruments. He took in exchange the one the man held and opened it.

It was a beautiful instrument. There was no needle, the whole dial revolving as he turned it about. Something he saw surprised him, for he frowned.

"That's curious," he said wonderingly; "are you sure this compass is true? The north should lie exactly over that flag-staff on the Commissioner's house—I tested it yesterday from this very—"

"Stuff!" interrupted the other loudly. "Rubbish; this compass has been verified; do you think I want to lead you astray—after the money I've sunk—"

On the morning before the expedition left, when the carriers were shouldering their loads, there came a brown-faced little man with a big white helmet over the back of his head and a fly whisk in his hand.

"Sanders, Commissioner," he introduced himself laconically," I've just come down from the interior; sorry I did not arrive before: you are going into the bush?"

"Yes."

"Diamonds, I understand?"

Sutton nodded.

"You'll find a devil of a lot of primitive opposition to your march. The Alebi people will fight you, and the Otaki folk will chop you, sure." He stood thinking, and swishing his whisk from side to side.

"Avoid trouble," he said, "I do not want war in my territories—and keep away from the Portuguese border."

Sutton smiled.

"We shall give that precious border a wide berth —the Colonial Office has seen the route, and approves."

The Commissioner nodded again and eyed Sutton gravely. "Good luck," he said.

The next day the expedition marched with the dawn, and disappeared into the wood beyond the Isisi River.

A week later the stout man sailed for England.

Months passed and none returned, nor did any news come of the expedition either by messenger, or by Lokali. A year went by, and another, and still no sign came.

Beyond the seas, people stirred uneasily, cablegram and letter, and official dispatch came to the Commissioner, urging him to seek for the lost expedition of the white men who had gone to find the River of Stars. Sanders of Bofabi shook his head.

What search could be made? Elsewhere, a swift little steamer following the courses of a dozen rivers, might penetrate—the fat water-jacket of a maxim gun persuasively displayed over the bow— into regions untouched by European influence, but the Alebi country was bush. Investigation meant an armed force; an armed force meant money— the Commissioner shook his head.

Nevertheless he sent two spies secretly into the bush, cunning men, skilled in woodcraft. They were absent about three months, and returned one leading the other.

"They caught him, the wild people of the Alebi," said the leader without emotion, "and put out his eyes: that night, when they would have burnt him, I killed his guard and carried him to the bush."

Sanders stood before his bungalow, in the green moonlight, and looked from the speaker to the blind man, who stood uncomplainingly, patiently twiddling his fingers.

"What news of the white men?" he asked at last, and the speaker, resting on his long spear, turned to the sightless one at his side.

"What saw you, Messambi?" he asked in the vernacular.

"Bones," croaked the blind man, "bones I saw; bones and nearly bones. They crucified the white folk in a big square before the chief's house, and there is no man left alive so men say."

"So I thought," said Sanders gravely, and made his report to England.

Months passed and the rains came and the green season that follows the rains, and Sanders was busy, as a West Central African Commissioner can be busy, in a land where sleeping sickness and tribal feuds contribute steadily to the death rate.

He had been called into the bush to settle a witch-doctor palaver. He travelled sixty miles along the tangled road that leads to the Alebi country, and established his seat of justice at a small town called M'Saga. He had twenty Houssa9 with him, else he might not have gone so far with impunity. He sat in the thatched palaver house and listened to incredible stories of witchcraft, 01 spells cast, of wasting sickness that fell in consequence, of horrible rites between moonset and sunrise, and gave judgment.

The witch-doctor was an old man, but Sanders had no respect for grey hairs.

"It is evident to me that you are an evil man," he said, "and—"

"Master!"

It was the complainant who interrupted him, a man wasted by disease and terror, who came into the circle of soldiery and stolid townspeople.

"Master, he is a bad man—"

"Be silent," commanded Sanders.

"He practises devil spells with white men's blood," screamed the man, as two soldiers seized him at a gesture from the Commissioner. "He keeps a white man chained in the forest—"

"Eh?"

Sanders was alert and interested. He knew natives better than any other man; he could detect a lie—more difficult an accomplishment, he could detect the truth. Now he beckoned the victim of the witch-doctor's enmity towards him.

"What is this talk of white men?" he asked.

The old doctor said something in a low tone, fiercely, and the informer hesitated.

"Go on," said Sanders.

"He says—"

"Go on!"

The man was shaking from head to foot.

"There is a white man in the forest—he came from the River of Stars—the Old One found him and put him in a hut, needing his blood for charms...."

The man led the way along a forest path, behind him came Sanders, and, surrounded by six soldiers, the old witch-doctor with his hands strapped together.

Two miles from the village was a hut. The elephant grass grew so high about it that it was scarcely visible. Its roof was rotten and sagging, the interior was vile...

Sanders found a man lying on the floor, chained by the leg to a heavy log; a man who laughed softly to himself, and spoke like a gentleman. The soldiers carried him into the open, and laid him carefully on the ground. His clothes were in tatters, his hair and his beard were long, there were many little scars on either forearm where the witch-doctor's knife had drawn blood.

"M—m," said Sanders, and shook his head.

"...The River of Stars," said the wreck, with a chuckle, "pretty name—what? Kimberley? Why, Kimberley is nothing compared to it... I did not believe it until I saw it with my eyes... the bed of the river is packed with diamonds, and you'd never find it, Lambaire, even with the chart, and your infernal compass... I've left a cache of tools, and food for a couple of years...."

He thrust his hand into his rag of a shirt and brought out a scrap of paper. Sanders bent down to take it, but the man pushed him back with his thin hand.

"No, no, no," he breathed. "You take the blood, that's your job—I'm strong enough to stand it—one day I'll get away..."

Ten minutes later he fell into a sound sleep. Sanders found the soiled paper, and put it into his uniform pocket.

He sent back to the boat and his men brought two tents which were pitched in a clearing near the hut. The man was in such a deplorable condition that Sanders dared not take the risk of moving him. That night, when the camp lay wrapped in sleep and the two native women whom the Commissioner had commanded to watch the sick man were snoring by their charge, the wreck woke. Stealthily he rose from bed and crept out into the starry night.

Sanders woke to find an empty hut and a handful of rags that had once been a white man's coat on the banks of the tiny forest stream, a hundred yards from the camp.

* * * * *

THE witch doctor of M'Saga, summoned to an early morning palaver, came in irons and was in no doubt as to the punishment which awaited him, for nearby in the forest the houssas had dug up much evidence of sacrifice.

"Master," said the man, facing the stare of grey eyes, "I see death in your face."

"That is God's truth," said Sanders, and hanged him then and there.

I. — AMBER

AMBER sat in his cell at Wellboro' gaol, softly whistling a little tune and beating time on the floor with his stockinged feet. He had pushed his stool near to the corrugated wall, and tilted it back so that he was poised on two of its three legs.

His eyes wandered round the little room critically.

Spoon and basin on the shelf; prison regulations varnished a dull yellow, above these; bed neatly folded... he nodded slowly, still whistling.

Above the bed and a little to the left was a small window of toughened glass, admitting daylight but affording, by reason of its irregular texture, no view of the world without. On a shelf over the bed was a Bible, a Prayer Book, and a dingy library book.

He made a grimace at the book; it was a singularly dull account of a singularly dull lady missionary who had spent twenty years in North Borneo without absorbing more of the atmosphere of that place than that it "was very hot" and further that native servants could be on occasion "very trying."

Amber was never fortunate with his library books. Five years ago, when he had first seen the interior of one of His Majesty's gaols, he had planned a course of study embracing Political Economy and the Hellenic Drama, and had applied for the necessary literature for the prosecution of his studies. He had been " served out" with an elementary Greek grammar and Swiss Family Robinson, neither of which was noticeably helpful. Fortunately the term of imprisonment ended before he expected; but he had amused himself by translating the adventures of the virtuous Swiss into Latin verse, though he found little profit in the task, and abandoned it.

During his fourth period of incarceration he made chemistry his long suit; but here again fortune deserted him, and no nearer could he get to his reading of the science than to secure the loan of a *Squire* and a *Materia Medica*.

Amber, at the time I describe, was between twenty-eight and thirty years of age, a little above medium height, well built, though he gave you the impression of slightness. His hair was a reddish yellow, his eyes grey, his nose straight, his mouth and chin were firm, and he was ready to show two rows of white teeth in a smile, for he was easily amused. The lower part of his face was now unshaven, which detracted from his appearance, but none the less he was, even in the ugly garb of his bondage, a singularly good-looking young man.

There was the sound of a key at the door, and he rose as the lock snapped twice and the door swung outward.

"75," said an authoritative voice, and he stepped out of the cell into the long corridor, standing to attention.

The warder, swinging his keys at the end of a bright chain, pointed to the prisoner's shoes neatly arranged by the cell door.

"Put 'em on."

Amber obeyed, the warder watching him.

"Why this intrusion upon privacy, my Augustus?" asked the kneeling Amber.

The warder, whose name was not Augustus, made no reply. In earlier times he would have " marked " Amber for insolence, but the eccentricities of this exemplary prisoner were now well-known, besides which he had some claim to consideration, for he it was who rescued Assistant Warder Beit from the fury of the London Gang. This had happened at Devizes County Gaol in 1906, but the prison world is a small one, and the fame of Amber ran from Exeter to Chelmsford, from Lewes to Strangeways.

He marched with his custodian through the corridor, down a polished steel stairway to the floor of the great hall, along a narrow stone passage to the Governor's office. Here he waited for a few minutes, and was then taken to the Governor's sanctum.

Major Bliss was sitting at his desk, a burnt little man with a small black moustache and hair that had gone grey at the temples.

With a nod he dismissed the warder.

"75," he said briefly, "you are going out tomorrow, on a Home Office order."

"Yes, sir," said Amber.

The Governor was thoughtfully silent for a moment, drumming his fingers noiselessly on his blotting-pad.

"What are you going to do?" he demanded suddenly.

Amber smiled.

"I shall pursue my career of crime," he said cheerfully, and the Governor frowned and shook his head.

"I can't understand you—haven't you any friends?"

Again the amused smile.

"No, sir," Amber was even more cheerful than before. "I have nobody to blame for my detection but myself."

The Major turned over some sheets of paper that lay before him, read them, and frowned again.

"Ten convictions!" he said. "A man of your capacity—why, with your ability you might have been—"

"Oh no, I mightn't," interrupted the convict, "that's the gag that judges work, but it's not true. It doesn't follow because a man makes an ingenious criminal that he would be a howling success as an architect, or because he can forge a cheque that he would have made a fortune by company promotion. An ordinary intelligent man can always shine in crime because he is in competition with very dull-witted and ignorant fellow craftsmen."

He took a step forward and leant on the edge of the desk.

"Look here, sir, you remember me at Sandhurst; you were a man of my year. You know that I was dependent on an allowance from an uncle who died before I passed through. What was I fit for when I came down? It seemed jolly easy the first week in London, because I had a tenner to carry on with.

But in a month I was starving. So I worked the Spanish prisoner fraud, played on the cupidity of people who thought they were going to make an immense fortune with a little outlay—it was easy money for me."

The Governor shook his head again.

"I've done all sorts of stunts since then," 75 went on unveraciously. "I've worked every kind of trick," he smiled as at some pleasant recollection. "There isn't a move in the game that I don't know; there isn't a bad man in London I couldn't write the biography of, if I was so inclined. I've no friends, no relations, nobody in the world I care two penn'oth of gin about, and I'm quite happy: and when you say I have been in prison ten times, you should say fourteen."

"You're a fool," said the Governor, and pressed a bell.

"I'm an adventuring philosopher," said 75 complacently, as the warder came in to march him back to his cell....

Just before the prison bell clanged the order for bed, a warder brought him a neat bundle of clothing.

"Look over these, 75, and check them," said the officer pleasantly. He handed a printed list to the prisoner.

"Can't be bothered," said Amber, taking the list. "I'll trust to your honesty."

"Check 'em."

Amber unfastened the bundle, unfolded his clothing, shook them out and laid them over the bed.

"You keep a man's kit better than they do in Walton," he said approvingly, "no creases in the coat, trousers nicely pressed—hullo, where's my eyeglass?"

He found it in the waistcoat pocket, carefully wrapped in tissue paper, and was warm in his praise of the prison authorities.

"I'll send a man in to shave you in the morning," said the warder and lingered at the door.

"75," he said, after a pause, "don't you come back here."

"Why not?"

Amber looked up with his eyebrows raised.

"Because this is a mug's game," said the warder. "A gentleman like you! Surely you can keep away from a place like this!"

Amber regarded the other with the glint of a smile in his eyes.

"You're ungrateful, my warder," he said gently. "Men like myself give this place a tone, besides which, we serve as an example to the more depraved and lawless of the boarders."

(It was an eccentricity of Amber's that he invariably employed the possessive pronoun in his address.)

Still the warder lingered.

"There's lots of jobs a chap like you could take up," he said, almost resentfully," if you only applied your ability in the right direction—"

75 raised his hand in dignified protest.

"My warder," he said gravely, "you are quotin' the Sunday papers, and that I will not tolerate, even from you."

Later, in the Warders' Mess, Mr. Scrutton said that as far as he was concerned he gave 75 up as a bad job."

"As nice a fellow as you could wish to meet," he confessed.

"How did he come down?" asked an assistant warder.

"He was a curate in the West End of London, got into debt and pawned the church plate—he told me so himself!"

There were several officers in the mess-room. One of these, an elderly man, removed his pipe before he spoke.

"I saw him in Lewes two years ago; as far as my recollection serves me, he was thrown out of the Navy for running a destroyer ashore."

Amber was the subject of discussion in the little dining-room of the Governor's quarters, where Major Bliss dined with the deputy governor.

"Try as I can," said the Governor in perplexity, I cannot remember that man Amber at Sandhurst —he says he remembers me, but I really cannot place him...."

Unconscious of the interest he was exciting, Amber slumbered peacefully on his thin mattress, smiling in his sleep.

*****

OUTSIDE the prison gates on the following morning was a small knot of people, mainly composed of shabbily dressed men and women, waiting for the discharge of their relatives.

One by one they came through the little wicket-gate, grinning sheepishly at their friends, submitting with some evidence of discomfort to the embraces of tearful women, receiving with greater aplomb the rude jests of their male admirers.

Amber came forth briskly. With his neat tweed suit, his soft Homburg hat and his eyeglass, those who waited mistook him for an officer of the prison and drew aside respectfully. Even the released prisoners, such as were there, did not recognize him, for he was clean-shaven and spruce; but a black-coated young man, pale and very earnest, had been watching for him, and stepped forward with outstretched hand.

"Amber?" he asked hesitatingly.

"Mr. Amber, "corrected the other, his head perked on one side like a curious hen.

"Mr. Amber." The missioner accepted the correction gravely. "My name is Dowles. I am a helper of the Prisoners' Regeneration League."

"Very interestin'—very interestin' indeed," murmured Amber, and shook the young man's hand vigorously. "Good work, and all that sort of thing, but uphill work, sir, uphill work."

He shook his head despairingly, and with a nod made as if to go.

"One moment, Mr. Amber." The young man's hand was on his arm. "I know about you and your misfortune—won't you let us help you?"

Amber looked down at him kindly, his hand rested on the other's shoulder.

"My chap," he said gently, "I'm the wrong kind of man: can't put me choppin' wood for a living, or find me a position of trust at 18s. a week. Honest toil has only the same attraction for me as the earth has for the moon; I circle round it once in twenty-four hours without getting any nearer to it—here!"

He dived his hand into his trousers pocket and brought out some money. There were a few sovereigns—these had been in his possession when he was arrested—and some loose silver. He selected half a crown.

"For the good cause," he said magnificently, and slipping the coin into the missioner's hand, he strode off.

II. — AT THE WHISTLERS

No. 46, Curefax Street, West Central, is an establishment which is known to a select few as "The Whistlers." Its official title is Pinnock's Club. It was founded in the early days of the nineteenth century by one Charles Pinnock, and in its day was a famous rendezvous.

That it should suffer the vicissitudes peculiar to institutions of the kind was inevitable, and its reputation rose and fell with the changing times. In 1889,1901, and again in 1903, it fell under suspicion, for in these years the club was raided by the police; though without any result satisfactory to the raiders.

It is indisputable that the habitués of the Whistlers were a curious collection of people, that it had few, if any, names upon the list of members of any standing in the social world; yet the club was popular in a shamefaced way. The golden youth of London delighted to boast, behind cautious hands, that they had had a night at the Whistlers; some of them hinted at high play; but the young gentlemen of fortune who had best reason for knowing the play was high indeed, never spoke of the matter, realizing, doubtlessly, that the world has little sympathy with a fool confessed, so that much of the evidence that an interfering constabulary desired was never forthcoming.

On a night in October the club was enjoying an unusual amount of patronage. Cab after cab set down well-dressed men before the decorous portals in Curefax Street. Men immaculately dressed, men a little over dressed, they came in ones and twos, and parties of three, at short intervals.

Some came out again after a short stay and drove off, but it seemed that the majority stayed. Just be ore midnight a taxi-cab drove up and discharged three passengers.

By accident or design, there is no outside light to the club, and the nearest electric standard is a few yards along the street, so that a visitor may arrive or depart in semi-darkness, and a watcher would find difficulty in identifying a patron.

In this case the chauffeur was evidently unacquainted with the club premises, and overshot the mark, pulling up within a few yards of the street lamp.

One of the passengers was tall and soldierly in appearance. He had a heavy black moustache, and the breadth of his shoulders suggested great muscular strength. In the light much of his military smartness vanished, for his face was puffed, and there were little bags under his eyes. He was followed by a shorter man who looked much younger than he was, for his hair, eyebrows and a little wisp of moustache were so fair as to be almost white. His nose and chin were of the character which for want of a better description may be called "nut-cracker," and down his face, from temple to chin, ran a long red scar.

Alphonse Lambaire was the first of these men, a remarkable and a sinister figure. Whether Lambaire was his real name or not I do not profess to know: he was English in all else. You might search in vain the criminal records of Scotland Yard without discovering his name, save in that section devoted to " suspected persons." He was a notorious character.

I give you a crude biography of him because he figures largely in this story. He was a handsome man, in a heavy unhealthy way, only the great diamond ring upon his little finger was a departure from the perfect taste of his ensemble.

The second man was "Whitey": what his real name was nobody ever discovered. "Whitey" he was to all; "Mr. Whitey " to the club servants, and " George Whitey " was the name subscribed to the charge sheet on the one occasion that the police made an unsuccessful attempt to draw him into their net.

The third was a boy of eighteen, fresh coloured, handsome, in a girlish fashion. As he stepped from the cab he staggered slightly and Lambaire caught his arm.

"Steady, old fellow," he said. Lambaire's voice was deep and rich, and ended in a little chuckle. "Pay that infernal brute, Whitey—pay the fare on the clock and not a penny more—here, hold up, Sutton my lad."

The boy made another blunder and laughed foolishly.

"We'll put him right in a minute, won't we, major?"

Whitey had a high little voice and spoke rapidly.

"Take his arm, Whitey," said Lambaire, "a couple of old brandies will make a new man of you..."

They disappeared through the swing doors of the club, and the hum of the departing taxi sounded fainter and fainter.

The street was almost deserted for a few minutes, then round the corner from St. James's Square came a motor-car. This driver also knew little of the locality, for he slowed down and came crawling along the street, peering at such numbers as were visible. He stopped before No. 46 with a jerk, jumped down from his seat and opened the door.

"This is the place, miss," he said respectfully, and a girl stepped out. She was very young and very pretty. She had evidently been spending the evening at a theatre, for she was dressed in evening finery, and over her bare shoulders an opera wrap was thrown.

She hesitated a moment, then ascended the two steps that led to the club, and hesitated again. Then she came back to the car.

"Shall I ask, miss?"

"If you please, John."

She stood on the pavement watching the driver as he knocked on the glass- panelled door. A servant came and held the door open, regarding the chauffeur with an unfriendly eye.

"Mr. Sutton—no, we've no such member."

"Tell him he's here as a guest," said the girl, and the waiter, looking over the head of the chauffeur, saw her and frowned.

"He's not here, madame," he said.

She came forward.

"He is here—I know he is here." Her voice was calm, yet she evidently laboured under some excitement. "You must tell him I want him—at once."

"He is not here, madame," said the man doggedly.

There was a spectator to the scene. He had strolled leisurely along the street, and had come to a standstill in the shadow of the electric brougham.

"He *is* here!" She stamped her foot. "In this wretched, wicked club—he is being robbed—it is wicked—wicked!"

The waiter closed the door in her face.

"Pardon me."

A young man, clean shaven, glass in eye, dressed in the neatest of tweed suits, stood by her, hat in hand. He had the happiest of smiles and a half-smoked cigarette lay on the pavement.

"Can I be of any assistance?"

His manner was perfect, respect, deference, apology, all were suggested by his attitude, and the girl in her distress forgot to be afraid of this providential stranger.

"My brother—he is there." She pointed a shaky finger at the bland door of the club. "He is in bad hands—I have tried..." Her voice failed her and her eyes were full of tears.

Amber nodded courteously. Without a word he led the way to her car, and she followed without question. She stepped in as he indicated.

"What is your address?—I will bring your brother."

With a hand that trembled, she opened a little bag of golden tissue that hung at her wrist, opened a tiny case and extracted a card.

He took it, read it, and bowed slightly.

"Home," he said to the driver, and stood watching the tail lights of the brougham disappear.

He waited, thinking deeply.

This little adventure was after his own heart. He had been the happiest man in London that day, and was on his way back to the modest Bloomsbury bed-sitting-room he had hired, when fortune directed his footsteps in the direction of Curefax Street.

He saw the car vanish from sight round a corner, and went slowly up the steps of the club. He pushed open the door, walked into the little hall-way, nodding carelessly to a stout porter who sat in a little box near the foot of the stairs.

The man looked at him doubtingly.

"Member, sir?" he asked, and was rewarded by an indignant stare.

"Beg pardon, sir," said the abashed porter. "We've got so many members that it is difficult to remember them."

"I suppose so," said Amber coldly. He mounted the stairs with slow steps; half-way up he turned.

"Is Captain Lawn in the club?"

"No, sir," said the man.

"Or Mr. Augustus Breet?"

"No, sir, neither of those gentlemen are in."

Amber nodded and continued on his way. That he had never heard of either, but that he knew both were out, is a tribute to his powers of observation. There was a rack in the hall where letters were displayed for members, and he had taken a brief survey of the board as he passed. Had there been any necessity, he could have mentioned half a dozen other members, but the porter's suspicions were lulled.

The first floor was taken up with dining and writing rooms. Amber smiled internally.

"This," he thought, "is where the gulls sign their little cheques—most thoughtful arrangement."

He mounted another flight of stairs, walked into a smoking-room where a number of flashily-dressed men were sitting, met their inquiring gaze with a nod and a smile directed at an occupied corner of the room, closed the door, and went up yet another and a steeper flight.

Before the polished portals of the room, which he gathered was the front room of the upper floor, a man sat on guard.

He was short and broad, his face was unmistakably that of a prize-fighter's, and he rose and confronted Amber.

"Well, sir?"

The tone was uncompromisingly hostile.

"All right," said Amber, and made to open the door.

"One moment, sir, you're not a member."

Amber stared at the man.

"My fellow," he said stiffly, "you have a bad memory for faces."

"I don't remember yours, anyway."

The man's tone was insolent, and Amber saw the end of his enterprise before ever it had begun.

He thrust his hands into his pockets and laughed quietly.

"I am going into that room," he said.j

"You're not."

Amber reached out his hand and grasped the knob of the door, and the man gripped him by the shoulder.

Only for a second, for the intruder whipped round like a flash.

The door-keeper saw the blow coming and released his hold to throw up a quick and scientific guard— but too late. A hard fist, driven as by an arm of steel, caught him under the point of the jaw and he fell back, missed his balance, and went crashing down the steep stairs—for this was the top flight and conveniently ladder-like.

Amber turned the door-handle and went in.

The players were on their feet with apprehensive eyes fixed on the door; the crash of the janitor's body as it struck the stairs had brought them up. There had been no time to hide the evidence of play, and cards were scattered about the floor and on the tables, money and counters lay in confusion....

For a moment they looked at one another, the calm man in the doorway and the scowling players at the tables. Then he closed the door softly behind him and came in. He looked round deliberately for a place to hang his hat.

Before they could question him the door-keeper was back, his coat off, the light of battle in his eye.

"Where is he?" he roared. "I'll learn him...."

His language was violent, but justified in the circumstances.

"Gentlemen," said Amber, standing with his back to the wall, "you can have a rough house, and the police in, or you can allow me to stay."

"Put him out!"

Lambaire was in authority there. His face was puckered and creased with anger, and he pointed to the trespasser.

"Put him out, George—"

Amber's hands were in his pockets.

"I shall shoot," he said quietly, and there was a silence and a move backward.

Even the pugilistic janitor hesitated.

"I have come for a quiet evening's amusement," Amber went on. "I'm an old member of the club, and I'm treated like a split*; most unfriendly!"

[* Thieves' argot for "detective."]

He shook his head reprovingly.

His eyes were wandering from face to face; he knew many who were there, though they might not know him. He saw the boy, white of face, limp, and half asleep, sprawling in a chair at Lambaire's table.

"Sutton," he said loudly, "Sutton, my buck, wake up and identify your old friend."

Gradually the excitement was wearing down. Lambaire jerked his head to the door-keeper and reluctantly he retired.

"We don't want any fuss," said the big man; he scowled at the imperturbable stranger. "We don't know you; you've forced your way in here, and if you're a gentleman you'll retire."

"I'm not a gentleman," said Amber calmly, "I'm one of yourselves."

He made his way to where the youth half sat, half lay, and shook him.

"I came to see my friend," he said, "and a jolly nice mess some of you people have made of him."

He turned a stern face to the crowd.

"I'm going to take him away," he said suddenly.

His strength was surprising, for with one arm he lifted the boy to his feet.

"Stop!"

Lambaire was between him and the door.

"You leave that young fellow here—and clear."

Amber's answer was characteristic.

With his disengaged hand, he lifted a chair, swung it once in a circle round his head, and sent it smashing through the window.

They heard the faint crackle of it as it struck the street below, the tinkle of falling glass, and then a police whistle.

Lambaire stood back from the door and flung it open.

"You can go," he said between his teeth. "I shall remember you."

"If you don't," said Amber, with his arm round the boy, "you've got a jolly bad memory."

III. — INTRODUCES PETER, THE ROMANCIST

AMBER had £86 10s.—a respectable sum.

He had an invitation to take tea with Cynthia Sutton at five o'clock in the afternoon. He had thought to hand the money to her on behalf of her brother—on second thoughts he decided to send the young man's losses to him anonymously. After all he was adjudging those losses by approximation. He had a pleasant room in Bloomsbury, a comfortable armchair, a long, thin, mild cigar and an amusing book, and he was happy. His feet rested on a chair, a clock ticked—not unmusically—it was a situation that makes for reverie, day-dreams, and sleep. His condition of mind might be envied by many a more useful member of society, for it was one of complete and absolute complaisance.

There came a knock at the door, and he bade the knocker come in. A neat maid entered with a tray, on which lay a card, and Amber took it up carelessly.

"Mr. George Whitey," he read. "Show him up."

Whitey was beautifully dressed. From his glossy silk hat to his shiny patent shoes, he was everything that a gentleman should be in appearance.

He smiled at Amber, placed his top-hat carefully upon the table, and skinned his yellow gloves.

Amber, holding up the card by the corner, regarded him benevolently.

When the door had shut—

"And what can I do for you, my Whitey?" he demanded.

Whitey sat down, carefully loosened the buttons of his frock-coat, and shot his cuffs.

"Name of Amber?"

His voice was a very high one; it was of a whistling shrillness.

Amber nodded.

"The fact of it is, old fellow," said the other, with easy familiarity," Lambaire wants an understanding, an undertaking, and—er—um—"

"And who is Lambaire?" asked the innocent Amber.

"Now, look here, dear boy," Whitey bent forward and patted Amber's knee, "let us be perfectly frank and above board. We've found out all about you —you're an old lag—you haven't been out of prison three days—am I right?"

He leant back with the triumphant air of a man who is revealing a well-kept secret.

"Bull's-eye," said Amber calmly. "Will you have a cigar or a butter dish?"

"Now we know you—d'ye see? We've got you taped down to the last hole. We bear no resentment, no malice, no nothing."

"No anything," corrected Amber. "Yes—?"

"This is our point." Whitey leant forward and traced the palm of his left hand with his right finger. "You came into the Whistlers—bluffed your way in—very clever, very clever—even Lambaire admits that—we overlook that; we'll go further and overlook the money."

He paused significantly, and smiled with some meaning.

"Even the money," he repeated, and Amber raised his eyebrows.

"Money?" he said. "My visitor, I fail to rise to this subtle reference." " The money," said Whitey slowly and emphatically, "there was close on a hundred pounds on Lambaire's table alone, to say nothing of the other tables. It was there when you came in-—it was gone when you left."

Amber's smile was angelic in its forgiveness. "May I suggest," he said, "that I was not the only bad character present?"

"Anyway, it doesn't matter, the money part of it," Whitey went on. "Lambaire doesn't want to prosecute."

"Ha! ha! " said Amber, laughing politely. "He doesn't want to prosecute; all he wants you to do is to leave young Sutton alone; Lambaire says that there isn't any question of making money out of Sutton, it's a bigger thing than that, Lambaire says—"

"Oh, blow Lambaire!" said Amber, roused to wrath. "Stifle Lambaire, my Whitey! he talks like the captain of the Forty Thieves. Go back to your master, my slave, and tell him young Ali Baba Amber is not in a condition of mind to discuss a workin' arrangement—"

Whitey had sprung to his feet, his face was unusually pale, his eyes narrowed till they were scarcely visible, his hands twitched nervously. "Oh, you—you know, do you?" he stuttered.

"I told Lambaire that you knew—that's your game, is it? Well, you look out!"

He wagged a warning finger at the astonished young man in the chair.

"You look out, Amber! Forty Thieves and Ali Baba, eh? So you know all about it—who told you? I told Lambaire that you were the sort of nut that would get hold of a job like this !"

He was agitated, and Amber, silent and watchful, twisted himself in his seat to view him the better, watching his every move. Whitey picked up his hat, smoothed it mechanically on the sleeve of his coat, his lips were moving as though he were talking to himself. He walked round the table that stood in the centre of the room, and made for the door.

Here he stood for a few seconds, framing some final message.

"I've only one thing to say to you," he said at last, "and that is this: if you want to come out of this business alive, go in with Lambaire— he'll share all right; if you get hold of the chart, take it to Lambaire. It'll be no use to you without the compass—see, an' Lambaire's got the compass, and Lambaire says—"

"Get out," said Amber shortly, and Whitey went, slamming the door behind him.

Amber stepped to the window and from the shadow of the curtain watched his visitor depart.

A cab was waiting for him, and he stepped in.

"No instructions for driver," noted Amber. "He goes home as per arrangement."

He rang a bell and a maid appeared.

"My servant," he said, regarding her with immense approval, "we will have our bill—nay, do not look round, for there is but one of us. When we said 'we,' we spoke in an editorial or kingly sense."

"Also," he went on gaily, "instruct our boots to pack our belongings—for we are going away."

The girl smiled.

"You haven't been with us long, sir," she said.

"A king's messenger," said Amber gravely, "never stays any length of time in one place; ever at the call of exigent majesty, burdened with the responsibilities of statescraft; the Mercury of Diplomacy, he is the nomad of civilization."

He dearly loved a pose, and now he strode up and down the room with his head on his breast, his hands clasped behind him, for the benefit of a Bloomsbury parlour-maid.

"One night in London, the next in Paris, the next grappling with the brigands of Albania, resolved to sell his life dearly, the next swimming the swollen waters of the Danube, his despatches between his teeth, and bullets striking the dark water on either side—"

"Lor!" said the startled girl, "you does have a time !"

"I does," admitted Amber; "bring the score, my wench."

She returned with the bill, and Amber paid, tipping her magnificently, and kissing her for luck, for she was on the pretty side of twenty-five.

His little trunk was packed, and a taxi-cab whistled for.

He stood with one foot upon the rubber-covered step, deep in thought, then he turned to the waiting girl.

"If there should come a man of unprepossessing appearance, whitish of hair and pallid of countenance, with a complexion suggestive of a whitewashed vault rather than of the sad lily—in fact if the Johnny calls who came in an hour ago, you will tell him I am gone."

He spoke over his shoulder to the waiting housemaid.

"Yes, sir," she said, a little dazed.

"Tell him I have been called away to—to Teheran."

"Yes, sir."

"On a diplomatic mission," he added with relish.

He stepped into the car, closing the door behind him.

An errand-boy, basket on arm, stood fascinated in the centre of the side- walk, listening with open mouth.

"I expect to be back," he went on, reflecting with bent head, "in August or September, 1943—you will remember that?"

"Yes, sir," said the girl, visibly impressed, and Amber, with a smile and a nod, turned to the driver.

"Home," he said.

"Beg pardon, sir?"

"Borough High Street," corrected Amber, and the car jerked forward.

He drove eastward, crossed the river at London Bridge, and dismissed the taxi at St. George's Church. With the little leather trunk containing his spare wardrobe, in his hand, he walked briskly up a broad street until he came to a narrow thoroughfare, which was bisected by a narrower and a meaner. He turned sharply to the left and walking as one who knew his way, he came to the dingiest of the dingy houses in that unhappy street.

19, Redcow Court, was not especially inviting. There was a panel missing from the door, the passage was narrow and dirty, and a tortuous broken flight of stairs ran crookedly to the floors above.

The house was filled with the everlasting noise of shrill voices, the voices of scolding women and fretful babies. At night there came a deeper note in the babel; many growling harsh-spoken men talked. Sometimes they would shout angrily, and there were sounds of blows and women's screams, and a frowsy little crowd, eager for sanguinary details, gathered at the door of No. 19.

Amber went up the stairs two at a time, whistling cheerfully. He had to stop half-way up the second flight because two babies were playing perilously on the uncarpeted stairway.

He placed them on a safer landing, stopped for a moment or two to talk to them, then continued his climb.

On the topmost floor he came to the door of a room and knocked.

There was no reply and he knocked again.

"Come in!" said a stern voice, and Amber entered.

The floor was scrubbed white, the centre was covered by a bright, clean patch of carpet, and a small gate-legged table exposed a polished surface. There were two or three pictures on the walls, ancient and unfashionable prints, representing mythological happenings. *Ulysses Returned* was one, *Perseus and the Gorgon* was another. *Prometheus Bound* was an inevitable third.

The song of a dozen birds came to Amber as he closed the door softly behind him. Their cages ran up the wall on either side of the opened window, the sill of which was a smother of scarlet geranium.

Sitting in a Windsor chair by the table was a man of middle age. He was bald-headed, his moustache and side whiskers were fiery red, and, though his eyebrows were shaggy and his eyes stern, his general appearance was one of extreme benevolence. His occupation was a remarkable one, for he was sewing, with small stitches, a pillow-case.

He dropped his work on to his knees as Amber entered.

"Hullo!" he said, and shook his head reprovingly. "Bad penny, bad penny—eh! Come in; I'll make you a cup of tea.":

He folded his work with a care that was almost feminine, placed it in a little work-basket, and went bustling about the room. He wore carpet slippers that were a little too large for him, and he talked all the time.

"How long have you been out?—More trouble ahead? keep thy hands from picking and stealing, and thy mouth free from evil speaking—tut, tut!"

"My Socrates," said Amber reproachfully.

"No, no, no!" the little man was lighting a fire of sticks, "nobody ever accused you of bad talk, as Wild Cloud says—never read that yarn, have you? You've missed a treat. *Denver Dad's Bid for Fortune, or the King of the Sioux*—pronounced *Soo*. It's worth reading. The twenty-fourth part of it is out to-day."

He chattered on, and his talk was about the desperate and decorative heroism of the Wild West. Peter Musk, such was his name, was a hero worshipper, a lover of the adventurous, and an assiduous reader of that type of romance which too hasty critics dismiss contemptuously as "dreadfuls." Packed away behind the bright cretonne curtains that hid his book-shelves were many hundreds of these stories, each of which had gone to the creation of the atmosphere in which Peter lived.

"And what has my Peter been doing all this long time?" asked Amber.

Peter set the cups and smiled, a little mysteriously.

"The old life," he said, "my studies, my birds, a little needlework—life runs very smoothly to a broken man an' a humble student of life."

He smiled again, as at a secret thought.

Amber was neither piqued nor amused by the little man's mystery, but regarded him with affectionate interest.

Peter was ever a dreamer. He dreamt of heroic matters such as rescuing grey-eyed damsels from tall villains in evening dress. These villains smoked cigarettes and sneered at the distress of their victims, until Peter came along and, with one well-directed blow, struck the sallow scoundrels to the earth.

Peter was in height some four feet eleven inches, and stoutish. He wore big, round, steel-rimmed glasses, and had a false tooth—a possession which ordinarily checks the pugilistically inclined, and can reasonably serve as an excellent excuse for prudent inaction in moments when the finger of heroism beckons frantically.

Peter moreover led forlorn hopes; stormed (in armour of an impervious character) breached fortresses under flights of arrows; planted tattered flags, shot-riddled, on bristling ramparts; and between whiles, in calmer spirit, was martyred for his country's sake, in certain little warlike expeditions in Central Africa.

Being by nature of an orderly disposition, he brought something of the method of his life into his dreams.

Thus, he charged at the head of his men, between 19, Redcow Court, and the fish-shop, in the morning, when he went to buy his breakfast haddock. He was martyred between the Borough and the Marshalsea Recreation Grounds, when he took a walk; was borne to a soldier's grave, amidst national lamentations, on the return journey, and did most of his rescuing after business hours.

Many years ago Peter had been a clerk in a city warehouse; a quiet respectable man, given to gardening. One day money was missing from the cashier's desk, and Peter was suspected. He was hypnotized by the charge, allowed himself to be led off to the police station without protest, listened as a man in a dream to the recital of the evidence against him—beautifully circumstantial evidence it was—and went down from the dock not fully realizing that a grey-haired old gentleman on the bench had awarded him six months' hard labour, in a calm unemotional voice.

Peter had served four months of his sentence when the real thief was detected, and confessed to his earlier crime. Peter's employers were shocked; they were good, honest, Christian people, and the managing director of the company was—as he told Peter afterwards—so distressed that he nearly put off his annual holiday to the Engadine.

The firm did a handsome thing, for they pensioned Peter off, paying him no less than 25s. a week, and Peter went to the Borough, because he had eccentric views, one of which was that he carried about him the taint of his conviction.

He came to be almost proud of his unique experience, boasted a little I fear, and earned an undeserved reputation in criminal circles. He was pointed out as he strolled forth in the cool of summer evenings, as a man who had burgled a bank, as What's-his-name, the celebrated forger. He was greatly respected.

"How did you get on?"

Amber was thinking of the little man's many lovable qualities when the question was addressed to him,

"Me—oh, about the same, my Peter," he said with a smile.

Peter looked round with an extravagant show of caution.

"Any difference since I was there?" he whispered.

"I think C. Hall has been repainted," said Amber gravely.

Peter shook his head in depreciation.

"I don't suppose I'd know the place now," he said regretfully; "is the Governor's room still off A. Hall?"

Amber made no reply other than a nod.

The little man poured out the tea, and handed a cup to the visitor.

"Peter," said Amber, as he stirred the tea slowly, "where can I stay?"

"Here?"

Peter's face lit up and his voice was eager.

Amber nodded.

"They're after you, are they?" the other demanded with a chuckle. "You stay here, my boy. I'll dress you up in the finest disguise you ever saw, whiskers an' wig; I'll smuggle you down to the river, an' we'll get you aboard—"

Amber laughed.

"Oh, my Peter!" he chuckled. "Oh, my lawbreaker! No, it's not the police—don't look so sad, you heartless little man—no, I'm avoiding criminals —real wicked criminals, my Peter, not petty hooks like me, or victims of circumstance like you, but men of the big mob—top hole desperadoes, my Peter, worse than Denver Dick or Michigan Mike or Settler Sam, or any of those gallant fellows."

Peter pointed an accusing finger.

"You betrayed 'em, an' they're after you," he said solemnly, "They've sworn a vendetta—"

Amber shook his head.

"I'm after them," he corrected, "and the vendetta swearing has been all on my side. No, my Peter, I'm Virtuous Mike—I'm the great detective from Baker Street, N.W. I want to watch somebody without the annoyance of their watchin' me."

Peter was interested.

His eyes gleamed through his spectacles, and his hands trembled in his excitement.

"I see, I see," he nodded vigorously. "You're going to frusterate 'em."

"'Frusterate' is the very word I should have used," said Amber.

IV. — LAMBAIRE NEEDS A CHART

LAMBAIRE had an office in the city, where he conducted a business. No man knew what the business was. There was a brass plate on the door which offered no solution other than that—

J. LAMBAIRE

(AND AT PARIS)

might be found within. He had callers, wrote and received letters, and disappeared at odd intervals, whither none knew, though " and at Paris " might be a plausible explanation.

Some said he was an agent, a vague description which might mean anything; others, a financier, though optimistic folk, with airy projects, requiring a substantial flotation, were considerably disappointed to find he had no money to spare for freakish and adventurous promotions.

So many strange people had offices in the city, with no apparent object, that Lambaire's business did not form the subject of too close an inquiry.

It was announced that once upon a time he had financed an expedition to Central Africa, and if this were true, there was every reason for his presence at No i, Flair Lane, E.C. Other men had financed similar expeditions, had established themselves in similar offices, and, through the years, had waited for some return for the money they had spent. Such was a matter of history.

Yet Lambaire had a business, and a very profitable business. He was known by his bankers to be a silver broker, by yet another banker to possess an interest in the firm of Flithenstein & Borris, a firm of printers; he had shares in a line of tramp steamers which had gained an unenviable reputation in shipping circles; he was interested, if truth be told, in a hundred and one affairs, small and large, legitimate or shady.

He owned a horse or two; obliging horses that won when he backed them, and were at the wrong end of the course when he did not.

Two days following the hasty departure of Amber, he was in his office. It was the luncheon hour, and he pulled on his gloves slowly. A smile lingered at the corners of his mouth, and there was a satisfied twinkle in his eye.

His secretary stood expectantly by the desk, mechanically sorting a sheaf of notes.

Mr. Lambaire walked slowly to the heavy door of his private room, then paused, with a show of irresolution.

"Perhaps it would be better to write to-night," he said dubiously. The secretary nodded, and depositing his papers on the desk, opened a note- book.

"Perhaps it would," said Lambaire, as though questioning himself. "Yes, it might as well be done to-night."

"Dear Sir " (he began, and the secretary scribbled furiously),—" Dear Sir, I have to acknowledge your letter *re* Great Forest Diamond Mine. Full stop. I understand your—er—annoyance—"

"Impatience?" suggested the secretary.

"Impatience," accepted the dictator," but the work is going forward. Full stop. Regarding your offer to take up further shares, comma, I have to inform you that my Board are—are—"

"Is," corrected the secretary.

"Is," continued Mr. Lambaire, "prepared to allow you the privilege, subject to the approval of our—"

"Its," said the secretary.

"Its brokers. Yours faithfully.

Lambaire lit a cigar.

"How's that?" he asked jovially.

"Very good, sir," said the secretary, rubbing his hands, "a good thing for the Board—"

"For me," said Mr. Lambaire, without embarrassment.

"I said the Board," said the pale-faced secretary, and chuckled at the subtlety of the humour.

Something was pleasing Lambaire to-day, and the secretary took advantage of the spell of good humour.

"About this letter; there have been all sorts of people here to-day," he said suggestively, and Lambaire, once more on his way to the door, looked round sharply.

"What the devil do you mean, Grene?" he demanded, all the joviality wiped from his face.

His subordinate shifted uneasily; he was on a delicate topic. Lambaire trusted him to a point; it was safe that he should confess his knowledge of Lambaire's affairs—up to that point.

"It is this African affair," said the clerk.

Lambaire stood by the door, his head sunk in thought.

"I suppose you told them—?"

"I told them the usual yarn—that our surveyor was visiting the property, and that we expected to hear from him soon. One chap—Buxteds' clerk —got a bit cheeky, and I—" he hesitated.

"Yes, and—?"

"He said he didn't believe we knew where the mine was ourselves."

Lambaire's smile was a trifle forced.

"Ridiculous," he said, without any great heartiness. "As if one could float a diamond mining company without knowing where the property is —absurd, isn't it, Grene?"

"Very, sir," said the secretary politely.

Lambaire still stood by the door.

"The map was in the prospectus, the mine is just on the edge—Etruri Forest—isn't that the name?"

The secretary nodded, watching him.

"Buxteds' man, eh?" Lambaire was perturbed, for Buxteds are the shadiest and the sharpest solicitors in London, and they did not love him.

"If Buxteds get to know," he stopped—" what I mean is that if Buxteds thought they could blackmail me—"

He went out, thinking deeply.

There is nothing quite as foolish as floating a company, and by specious advertising to attract the money of the speculating public, when the very *raison d'être* of the company is non-existent. If there is one thing in the world that is necessary for the prosperity of a diamond mining company it is a diamond mine, and there were reasons why that couldn't be included in the assets of the company. The first reason was that Lambaire did not know within a hundred leagues where the property was situated; the second—and one not without importance—he possessed no certain knowledge that he had the right to dispose of the property, even if he knew where it was.

Yet Lambaire was not the type of enthusiast who floats diamond mines on no more solid basis than his optimism. To be perfectly candid, the Great Forest Diamond Mining Company had come into existence at a period when his cash balance was extremely low; for all the multiplicity of his interests, such periods of depression came to him. It may be said of him, as it was said, that he did not go to allotment until he realized that there was some doubt about the possibility of ever discovering this mine of his.

That it was a dream mine, the merest rumour of an Eldorado, unconfirmed save by the ravings of a dying man, and a chart which he did not possess, and by no means could secure, he did not admit in the florid little prospectus which was distributed privately, but thoroughly, to the easy investors of Britain. Rather he suggested that the mine was located and its rights acquired. The prospectus had dealt vaguely with " certain difficulties of transport which the company would overcome," and at the end came a learned and technical report from the "resident engineer" (no name), who spoke of garnets, and "pipes," and contained all the conversational terminology of such reports.

No attempt need be made to disguise the fact that Lambaire was without scruple. Few men are wholly bad, but, reading his record, one is inclined to the judgment that such good seed as humanity had implanted within him never germinated.

He had descended to the little vestibule of the building, and was stepping into the street without, when a taxi-cab drove up and deposited the dapper Whitey.

"I want you," he piped.

Lambaire frowned.

"I haven't any time—" he began.

"Come back," urged Whitey, catching his arm, "come back into the office; I've got something important to say to you."

Reluctantly the big man retraced his steps.

Mr. Secretary Grene had a narrow shave, for he was examining a private drawer of his employers when the footsteps of the men sounded in the stone-flagged corridor without.

With an agility and deftness that would have delighted Lambaire, had these qualities been exercised on his behalf, instead of being to his detriment, the secretary closed and locked the drawer with one motion, slipped the key into his pocket, and was busily engaged in reading his notes when the two entered.

"You can go, Grene," said Lambaire. "I've got a little business to transact with Mr. White— have your lunch and come back in half an hour."

When the door had closed on the secretary, Lambaire turned to the other.

"Well?" he demanded.

Whitey had taken the most comfortable chair in the room, and had crossed his elegantly cased legs. He had the pleasant air of one who by reason of superior knowledge was master of the situation.

"When you have finished looking like a smirking jackass, perhaps you will tell me why you have made me postpone my lunch," said Lambaire unpleasantly.

Whitey's legs uncurled, and he sat up.

"This is news, Lambaire." His impressive hand, upraised, emphasized the importance of the communication he had to convey.

"It's an idea, and news together," he said. "I've seen the Suttons."

Lambaire nodded. The audacity of Whitey was a constant surprise to him, but it was the big man's practice never to betray that surprise.

Whitey was obviously disappointed that his great tidings had fallen so flat.

"You take a dashed lot for granted," he grumbled. "I've seen the Suttons, Lambaire—seen 'em after the affair at the Whistlers; it wanted a bit of doing."

"You're a good chap, Whitey," soothed Lambaire, "a wonderful chap; well?"

"Well," said the ruffled man in the chair, "I had a talk with the boy—very sulky, very sulky> Lambaire; huffy, didn't want to have any truck with me; and his sister—phew !"

He raised his two hands, palms outwards, as he recalled the trying interview.

"She gave me the Ice," he said earnestly, "she was Cold—she was Zezo; talking to her, Lambaire, was like sitting in a draught! Br-r!" He shivered.

"Well, what about the boy?"

Whitey smiled slyly.

"Huffish, haughty, go to—you know where—but reasonable. He's got the hang of the Whistler. It was like catching a kicked cat to get him back. He put on his dam' Oxford and Eton dressing—haw—haw!—*you* know the voice. Awfully sorry, but the acquaintance had better drop—he'd made a mistake; no thank you, let the matter drop; good morning, mind the step."

Whitey was an indifferent mimic, but he conveyed the sense of the interview. "But he couldn't shake me—I was a sticker, I was the boy on the burning deck; he opened the door for me to go out, and I admired his geraniums; he rang the bell for a servant, and I said I didn't mind if I did; he fumed and fretted, walked up and down the room with his hands in his pockets; he told me what he thought of me and what he thought of you."

"What does he think of me?" said Lambaire quickly.

"I'd rather not say," said Whitey, "you'd be flattered—I don't think. He thinks you are a gentleman—no I Don't mind about a trifle like that. I sat down and argued with him. He said you were evidently the worst kind of waster."

"What did you say to that?" demanded Lambaire with a frown.

"I denied that," said Whitey virtuously. "'Not the worst kind,' I said; anyway, the interview ended by his promising to come up here this afternoon."

Lambaire paced the room in thought.

"What good will that do?" he asked.

Whitey raised imploring eyes to heaven.

"Hear me," he said, addressing an invisible deity. "Hark to him. I spend all the morning working for him, and he wants to know what is the good." He got up slowly and polished his hat with his sleeve.

"Here, don't go," said Lambaire, "I want to know a lot more. Now what is he prepared to do?"

"Look here, Lambaire," Whitey dropped all pretence at deference and geniality, and turned on the other with a snarl. "This kid can get at the chart. This diamond mine of ours has got to be more tangible than it is at present or there is going to be trouble; things are going rotten, and you know it."

"And suppose he won't part with it?"

"It is not a question of his parting with it," said Whitey; "he hasn't got it; it is his sister who has it. He's his father's son, you've got to remember that. You can bet that somewhere, tucked away out of sight inside him, he's got the old adventure blood; these sort of things don't die out. Look at me; my father was a—"

"Don't get off the subject," said Lambaire impatiently. "What are you driving at, Whitey? What does it matter to me whether he's got adventure blood, or lunatic blood, or any other kind of blood—he's got the chart that his father made, that was found on him when he died and was sent to the daughter by some fool of a Commissioner—eh? *That's* what we want!"

He rose jerkily, thrust his hands into his trousers pockets, and peeked his head forward, a mannerism of his when he was excited.

Though nominally Whitey was Lambaire's jackal, runner, general man of affairs and dependant, it was easy to see that the big man stood in some fear of his servant, and that there were moments when Whitey took charge and was not to be lightly ignored. Now it was that he was the bully, and overbearing, masterful director of things. With his high thin voice, his vehemence as he hissed and spluttered, he was a little uncanny, terrifying. He possessed a curious vocabulary, and strangely unfamiliar figures of speech. To illustrate his meaning he brought vivid if incongruous picture words to his aid. Sometimes they were undisguised slang words, culled from other lands—Whitey was something of a traveller and had cosmopolitan tastes.

"You're a Shining Red Light, Lambaire," he went on in furious flow of words. "People are getting out of your road; the Diamond business has got to be settled at once. Let people get busy, and they won't be content with finding out that the mine is minus; they'll want to know about the silver business and the printing business, and they'll put two and two together—d'ye see that? You was a fool ever to tackle the diamond game. It was the only straight deal you was ever in, but you didn't work it straight. If you had, you'd have got Sutton back alive; but no, you must have a funny compass, so that he could find the mine and make a chart of the road and only you could find it! Oh, you're a Hog of Cleverness, but you've overdone it!"

He grew a little calmer.

"Now look here," he went on, "young Sutton's coming to-day, and you've got to be Amiable; you've got to be Honest; you've got to be Engaging; you've got to Up and say 'Look here, old man, let's put all our cards on the table—'"

"I'll be cursed if I do," snapped Lambaire; "you're mad, Whitey. What do you think I'm—"

"'All the cards on the table'," repeated Whitey slowly, and rapped the desk with his bony knuckles to point each word, "your own pack, Lambaire; you've got to say, 'Look here, old son, let's understand one another; the fact of the matter is, etc., etc.'"

What the etc. was Whitey explained in the course of a heated, caustic and noisy five minutes.

At the end of that time Grene appeared on the scene, and the conversation came to an abrupt finish.

"Three o'clock," said Whitey, at the bottom of the stairs, "you play your cards well, and you get yourself out of a nasty mess."

Lambaire grunted an ungracious rejoinder and they parted.

It was a different Whitey who made an appearance at the appointed hour. An urbane, deferential, unruffled man, who piloted a youth to the office of J. Lambaire.

Francis Sutton was a good-looking boy, though the scowl that he thought it necessary to wear for the occasion disfigured him.

Yet he had a grievance, or the shreds of one, for he had the uncomfortable feeling that he had been tricked and made a fool of, and generally ill- treated.

It had been made clear to him that when that man of the world, Lambaire, had showed a preference for his society, had invited him to dinner, and had introduced him more than once to the Whistlers, it was not because the " financier" had taken a sudden fancy to him—not even because Lambaire had known his father in some far-off time—but because Lambaire wanted to get something out of him.

By what means of realization this had come to him it is no province of mine to say. The sweetest, the dearest, the most tender of woman being human, for all her fragrant qualities, may, in some private moment, be sufficiently human to administer a rebuke in language sufficiently convincing to bring a foolish young man to his senses.

The scowl was on his face when he came into Lambaire's private office. Lambaire was sitting at his big desk, which was Uttered with the mechanism of commerce to an unusual extent. There was a fat account-book open on the table before him, letters lay stacked in piles on either hand, and his secretary sat, with open note-book, by his side.

An imposing cheque-book was displayed before him, and he was very busy indeed when Whitey ushered his charge into this hive of industry.

"Ah, Mr. Sutton!" he said, answering with a genial smile the curt nod of the other, "glad to see you. Make Mr. Sutton comfortable, White—I've one or two things to finish off."

"Perhaps," said the young man, relaxing a "if I came a little later—?"

"Not at all, not at all."

Lambaire dismissed the supposition that he was too deeply employed to see him at once with a wave of the hand.

"Sit down," he pleaded, "only for one moment. Are you ready, Grene?"

"Yes, sir."

"Dear sir," dictated Lambaire, leaning back in his padded chair, "we have pleasure in enclosing a cheque for four thousand six hundred and twenty-five pounds seven and fourpence, in payment of half-yearly dividends. Full stop. We regret that we were not able to allot you any shares in our new issue; the flotation was twenty times over-subscribed. Yours, etc. Got that?"

" Yes, sir," said the unmoved Grene. Could this be the adventurer his sister had pictured? thought the young man. Would a man of this type stoop to lure him to a gaming house for the gain of his few hundreds?

"Send a cheque to Coutts —how much is it?" said Lambaire.

"About six thousand," said Grene at random.

"And pay that little account of mine at Fells— it's about four hundred—these wretched little wine bills mount up."

The latter portion of the sentence was addressed to Sutton, who found himself smiling sympathetically. As for Whitey, he was one benign grin.

"Now I think that is all," and Lambaire fluttered a few papers. "Oh, here is a letter from S—" He handed what was in reality a peremptory demand for the payment of the very wine bill to which he referred to Grene.

"Tell him I am sorry I cannot go to Cowes with him—I hate strange yachts, and unfortunately," this to the young man and with a smile of protest, "I cannot afford to keep my yacht as I did a few years ago. Now." He swung round in his seat as the door closed behind Grene.

"Now, Mr. Sutton, I want a straight talk with you; you don't mind White being here, do you? he's my confidant in most matters."

"I don't mind anybody," said the youth, though he was obviously ill at ease, not knowing exactly what was the object of the interview.

Lambaire toyed with a celluloid ruler before he began.

"Mr. Sutton," he said slowly, "you were at school, I think, when your father went to West Africa?"

"I was going up to Oxford," said the boy quickly.

Lambaire nodded.

"You know I equipped the expedition that had such an unfortunate ending?"

"I understood you had something to do with it."

"I had," said Lambaire, "it cost me—however, that has nothing to do with the matter. Now, Mr. Sutton, I am going to be frank with you. You are under the impression that I sought your acquaintance with some ulterior motive. You need not deny it; I had a—a—"

"Hunch," said the silent Whitey suddenly.

"I had what Mr. White calls a 'hunch' that this was so. I know human nature very well, Mr. Sutton; and when a man thinks badly of me, I know the fact instinctively."

To be exact, the intuition of Mr. Lambaire had less to do with his prescience than the information Whitey had been able to supply.

"Mr. Sutton, I'm not going to deny that I did have an ulterior motive in seeking your society." Lambaire leant forward, his hands on his knees, and was very earnest. "When your father—"

"Poor father," murmured Whitey.

"When your poor father died, a chart of his wanderings, showing the route he took, was sent to you, or rather to your sister, she being the elder. It was only by accident, during the past year, that I heard of the existence of that chart and I wrote to your sister for it."

"As I understand it, Mr. Lambaire," said Sutton, "you made no attempt to seek us out after my father's death; though you were in no sense responsible for his fate, my sister felt that you might have troubled yourself to discover what was happening to those who were suddenly orphaned through the expedition."

This tall youth, with his clear-cut effeminate face, had a mouth that drooped a little weakly. He was speaking now with the assurance of one who had known all the facts on which he spoke for years, yet it was the fact that until that morning, when his sister had given him some insight into the character of the man she distrusted, he had known nothing of the circumstances attending his father's death.

All the time he spoke Lambaire was shaking his head slowly, in melancholy protest at the injustice.

"No, no, no," he said, when the other had finished, "you're wrong, Mr. Sutton—I was ill at the time; I knew that you were all well off—"

"Ahem!" coughed Whitey, and Lambaire realized that he had made a mistake.

"So far from being well off—however, that is unimportant; it was only last year that, by the death of an uncle, we inherited—but rich or poor, that is beside the question."

"It is indeed," said Lambaire heartily. He was anxious to get away from ground that was palpably dangerous. "I want to finish what I had to say. Your sister refused us the chart; well and good, we do not quarrel with her, we do not wish to take the matter to law; we say 'very good—we will leave the matter,' although," he wagged his finger at the boy solemnly, "although it is a very serious matter for me, having floated—"

"Owing to your wishing to float," said Whitey softly.

"I should say wishing to float a company on the strength of the chart; still, I say, 'if the young lady feels that way, I'm sorry—I won't bother her'; then an idea struck me!" He paused dramatically. "An idea struck me—the mine which your father went to seek is still undiscovered; even with your chart, to which, by the way, I do not attach a great deal of importance—"

"It is practically of no value except to the owner," interrupted Whitey.

"No value whatever," agreed Lambaire; "even with the chart, any man who started out to hunt for my mine would miss it—what is required is—is—"

"The exploring spirit," Whitey put in. "The exploring spirit, born and bred in the bones of the man who goes out to find it. Mr. Sutton," Lambaire rose awkwardly, for he was heavily built, "when I said I sought you from ulterior motives, I spoke the truth. I was trying to discover whether you were the man to carry on your father's work—Mr. Sutton, you are !"

He said this impressively, dramatically, and the boy flushed with pleasure.

He would have been less than human if the prospect of such an expedition as Lambaire's words suggested did not appeal to him. Physically and mentally he bore no resemblance to Sutton the explorer, the man of many expeditions, but there was something of his father's intense curiosity in his composition, a curiosity which lies at the root of all enterprise.

In that moment all the warnings of his sister were unheeded, forgotten. The picture of the man she had drawn faded from his mind, and all he saw in Lambaire was a benefactor, a patron, and a large-minded man of business. He saw things more clearly (so he told himself) without prejudice (so he could tell his sister); these things had to be looked at evenly, calmly. The past, with the privations, which, thanks to his sister's almost motherly care and self-sacrifice, he had not known or felt, was dead.

"I—I hardly know what to say," he stammered; "of course I should like to carry on my father's work most awfully—I've always been very keen on that sort of thing, exploring and all that...."

He was breathless at the prospect which had unexpectedly been opened up to him. When Lambaire extended a large white hand, he grasped and shook it gratefully—he, who had come firm in the resolve to finally end the acquaintance.

"He's butter," said Whitey afterwards, "keep him away from the Ice and he's Dead Easy. It's the Ice that's the difficulty.

He shook his head doubtfully.

V. — AMBER ADMITS HIS GUILT

AND there was an end to it.

So Francis Sutton informed his sister with tremendous calm.

She stood by the window, drawing patterns with the tips of her fingers on the polished surface of a small table, and her eyes were fixed on the street without.

Francis had been illogical and unnecessarily loud in his argument, and she had been beaten down by the erratic and tumbling waves of his eloquence. So she remained quiet, and when he had finished talking for the fifth time, he resentfully remarked upon her sulky silence.

"You haven't given me a chance of speaking, Francis, and I am absolutely bewildered by your change of attitude—"

"Look here, Cynthia," he broke in impatiently, "it's no good your opening up this wretched subject again—Lambaire is a man of the world, we can't judge him by convent codes, or by schoolgirl codes; if you argue the matter from now until quarter-day you won't budge me. I'm going through with this. It's a chance that will never come again. I'm sure father would have liked it."

He paused expectantly, but she did not accept the lull as an opportunity.

"Now, for goodness sake, Cynthia, do not, I beg of you, sulk."

She turned from her contemplation of the outside world.

"Do you remember how you came home the other night?" she asked suddenly, and the boy's face went red.

"I don't think that's fair," he said hotly, "a man may make a fool of himself—"

"I wasn't going to speak of that," she said, "but I want to remind you that a gentleman brought you home—he knew Lambaire better than you or I know him—yes?—you were going to say something?"

"Go on," said the youth, a note of triumph in his voice, "I have something to say upon that subject."

"He said that Lambaire was something worse than a man about town—that he was a criminal, one of the cleverest of criminals, a man without scruple or pity."

There was a smile on Sutton's face when she finished.

"And do you know who this gentleman was?" he asked in glee. "He's Amber—you've never heard of Amber?"

She shook her head.

"He's a thief, just a low-down thief—you can jolly well shake your head, Cynthia, but he's a fellow who gets his living by his wits; he's been out of gaol exactly a week—that is your Mr. Amber."

"Mr. Amber," repeated a voice at the door, as a maid admitted the imperturbable subject of the conversation.

Amber was in the conventional garb of civilization. His tightly-buttoned morning coat was of the newest cut, his linen was of the shiniest. The hat which he held in his hand shone as only a new silk hat can shine, and spotless white was alike the colour of the spats over his varnished shoes and the skin-tight gloves on his hands.

He might have stepped out of a fashion plate, so immaculate was he.

He smiled cheerfully at the uncomfortable youth and held out his hand to the girl.

"Called in," he said easily, "passin' this way: motor 'buses pass the door—very convenient; what I like about London is the accessibility of everywhere to everywhere else—may I put my hat down? —thank you so much. If ever I make a lot of money I shall live in Park Lane; it's so close to the tube. And how are you?"

Sutton muttered an ungracious platitude and made for the door.

"One moment, Francis," the girl had gone red and white by turn, and the hand that traced patterns on the table had trembled a little when Amber came in: now she was very self-possessed, albeit paler than usual. The boy stopped, one hand on the handle of the door, and frowned warningly at his sister.

"Mr. Amber," she said, ignoring the signal, "I think it is only fair to you to repeat something I have just heard."

"I beg of you, Cynthia!" said Sutton angrily.

"It has been said, Mr. Amber," she continued, "that you are—are a bad character."

"My lady," said Amber, with a grave face, "I am a bad character."

"And—and you have recently been released from prison," she faltered, avoiding his eyes.

"If," said Amber carefully, "by 'recent' you mean nearly a week ago—that also is true."

"I told you," cried Sutton, with an exultant laugh, and Amber whipped round.

"My Democritus, my Abderite," he said reproachfully, "wherefore rollick? It is not so funny, this prison—*quid rides**, my Sutton?" His eyebrows rose questioningly.

> [* Latin: an allusion to Horace's *Quid rides? Mutato nomine de te fabula narratur* - What are you laughing at? Just change the name and the joke's on you.]

Something made the girl look at him. She may have expected to see him shamefaced; instead, she saw only righteous annoyance.

"My past misfortune cannot interest you, My Lady," he said a little sadly, "when, on a memorable night, I faced Janus, at your wish, entering the portals of an establishment to which I would not willingly invite a self-respecting screw—by which I mean the uniformed instrument of fate, the prison warder—I do not remember that you demanded my credentials, nor set me a test piece of respectability to play."

Then he again addressed himself to the boy.

"Mr. Sutton," he said softly, "methinks you are a little ungracious, a little precipitate: I came here to make, with the delicacy which the matter demanded, all the necessary confession of previous crimes, dodges, acts of venal artfulness, convictions, incarcerations, together with an appendix throwing light upon the facility with which a young and headstrong subaltern of cavalry might descend to the Avernus which awaits the reckless layer of odds on indifferent horses."

He said all this without taking breath, and was seemingly well satisfied with himself and the sketch he gave of his early life. He pulled himself erect, squared his shoulders and set his monocle more firmly in his eye, then with a bow to the girl, and an amused stare at the young man, he turned to the door.

"One moment, Mr. Amber," she found her voice, "I cannot allow you to go like this; we owe you something, Francis and I..."

"Owe me a memory," said Amber in a low voice, "that would be a pleasant reward, Miss Sutton."

Impulsively she stepped forward and held out her hand, and he took it.

"I'm so sorry," was all she said, but she knew by the pressure on her hand that he understood.

As they stood there, for the briefest space of time, hand to hand, Sutton slipped from the room, for he had been expecting visitors, and had heard the distant thrill of a bell.

Neither noticed his absence.

The girl's face was upraised to Amber's, and in her eyes was infinite compassion.

"You are too good—too good for that life," she said, and Amber shook his head, smiling with his eyes.

"You don't know," he said gently, "perhaps you are wasting your pity—you make me feel a scoundrel when you pity me."

50

Before she could reply the door was flung open, and Sutton burst into the room; behind him was Lambaire, soberly arrayed, sleek of hair and perfectly groomed, and no less decorous of appearance was the inevitable Whitey bringing up the rear.

Cynthia Sutton gazed blankly at the new-comers. It was a bold move of her brother's to bring these men to her house. Under any circumstances their reception would have been a stiff one; now, a cold anger took possession of her, for she guessed that they had been brought to complete the rout of Amber.

The first words of Sutton proved this.

"Cynthia," he said, with a satisfaction which he did not attempt to conceal, "these are the gentlemen that Mr. Amber has vilified—perhaps he would care to repeat—"

"Young, very young," said Amber tolerantly. He took the management of the situation from the girl's hands, and for the rest of the time she was only a spectator. "*Ne puero gladium—eh?*"*

[* Latin: Do not entrust a sword to a boy.]

He was the virtuous schoolmaster reproaching youth.

"And here we have evidence," he exhibited Lambaire and his companion with a sweep of his hand, "confronted by the men he has so deeply wronged; and now, my Lambaire, what have you to say about us that we have not already revealed?" " I know you are a thief," said Lambaire. "True, O King!" admitted Amber genially. "I know you've been convicted three or four times for various crimes."

"Sounds like a nursery rhyme," said Amber admiringly, "proceed, my Lambaire."

"That is quite enough, I think, to freeze you out of decent society."

"More than enough—much more than enough," confessed the unabashed young man, with a melancholy smile, "and what says my Whitey, eh? What says my pallid one?" " Look here, Amber," began Whitey. "I once had occasion to inform you," interrupted Amber severely, "that under no circumstances were you to take liberties with my name; I am Mister Amber to you, my Whitey."

"Mister or Master, you're a hook—" said the other.

"A what?"

The horrified expression on Amber's face momentarily deceived even so experienced a man as Whitey.

"I mean you are a well-known thief," he said.

"That is better," approved Amber, "the other is a coarse expression which a gentleman of parts should never permit himself to employ, my Boswell; and what else are we?"

"That's enough, I think," said the man rudely.

"Now that you mention the fact, I think that 'enough' is the word," he looked round the group, from face to face, with the quizzical smile that was seldom absent. "More than enough," he repeated. "We are detected, undone, frus-ter-ated, as a dear friend of mine would say."

He slowly unbuttoned his tight-fitting morning coat and thrust his hands into an inside pocket. With a great show of deliberation, he produced a gaudy pocket-book of red morocco. With its silver fittings, it was sufficiently striking to attract attention, even to those who had never seen it before. But there was one who knew it, and Lambaire made a quick step forward and snatched at it.

"That is mine!" he cried; but Amber was too quick for him.

"No, no, my Lambie," he said, "there is a lady here; let us postpone our horseplay for another occasion."

"That is mine," cried Lambaire angrily, "it was stolen the night you forced your way into the Whistlers. Mr. Sutton, I am going to make an example of this fellow. He came out of gaol last week, he goes back to-day; will you send for a policeman?"

The boy hesitated.

"Save you the trouble—save you the scandal— club raid and all that sort of thing," said Amber easily. "Here is your *portmanie*—you will find the money intact." He handed over the pocket-book with a pleasant little nod.

"I have retained," he went on, "partly as a reward for my honesty, partly as a souvenir of a pleasant occasion, one little fiver— commission— eh?"

He held between^his fingers a bank-note, and crackled it lovingly, and Cynthia, looking from one to the other in her bewilderment, saw Lambaire's face go grey with fear.

VI. — IN FLAIR COURT

NO word was spoken by Lambaire or Whitey as a taxi-cab carried them through the city to the big man's office. They had taken a hurried and disjointed farewell of Sutton and had left immediately after Amber.

It was after business hours, and Grene had gone, when Lambaire snapped the lock of his private room behind him, and sank into his padded lounge chair.

"Well, what do you think?"

Whitey looked down at him keenly as he put the question.

"Phew!" Lambaire wiped his forehead.

"Well?" demanded Whitey sharply.

"Whitey—that fellow's got us."

Whitey's thin lips curled in a contemptuous smile.

"You're dead easy to beat, Lambaire," he said in his shrill way, "you're Flab! You're a Jellyfish!"

He was lashing himself into one of his furies, and Lambaire feared Whitey in those moods more than he feared anything in the world.

"Look here, Whitey, be sensible; we've got to face matters; we've got to arrange with him, square him!"

"Square him!" Whitey's derision and scorn was in his whistling laugh. "Square Amber—you fool! Don't you see he's honest! He's honest, that fellow, and don't forget it."

"Honest—why—"

"Honest, honest, honest!" Whitey beat the desk with his clenched fist with every word. "Can't you see, Lambaire, are you blind? Don't you see that the fellow can be a lag and honest—that he can be a thief and go straight—he's that kind."

There was a long silence after he had finished. Whitey went over to the window and looked out; Lambaire sat biting his finger nails.

By and by Whitey turned.

"What is the position?" he asked.

The other shrugged his shoulders.

"Things are very bad; we've got to go through with this diamond business: you're a genius,

Whitey, to suggest the boy; if we send him to carry out the work, it will save us."

"Nothing can save us," Whitey snapped. "We're in a mess, Lambaire; it's got beyond the question of shareholders talkin', or an offence under the Companies Act—it's felony, Lambaire."

He saw the big man shiver, and nodded.

"Don't let us deceive ourselves," Whitey kept up a nodding of head that was grotesquely reminiscent of a Chinese toy, "it's twenty years for you, and twenty years for me; the police have been searching the world for the man that can produce those banknotes—and Amber can put 'em wise."

Again a long silence. A silence that lasted for the greater part of an hour; as the two men sat in the gathering darkness, each engaged with his own thoughts.

It was such an half-hour that any two guilty men, each suspicious of the other, might spend. Neither the stirrings of remorse nor the pricking of conscience came into their broodings. Crude schemes of self-preservation at any cost—at whose expense they cared not—came in irregular procession to their minds.

Then—" You've got nothing here, I suppose?" said Whitey, breaking the long silence.

Lambaire did not answer at once, and his companion repeated the question more sharply. "No—yes," hesitated Lambaire, "I've got a couple of plates—"

"You fool," hissed the other, "you hopeless Mug!

Here! Here in the first place they'd search—"

"In my safe, Whitey," said the other, almost pleadingly, "my own safe; nobody has a key but me."

There was another long silence, broken only by the disconnected hissings of Whitey.

"To-morrow—we clear 'em out, d'ye hear, Lambaire; I'd rather be at the mercy of a Nut like Amber, than have my life in the hands of a fool like you. An' how have you got the plates? Wrapped up in a full signed confession, I'll take my oath! Little tit-bits about the silver business, eh? An' the printing establishment at Hookley, eh? Full directions and a little diagram to help the Splits— oh, you funny fool!"

Lambaire was silent under the tirade. It was nearly dark before Whitey condescended to speak again.

"There's no use our sitting here," he said roughly. "Come and have some dinner, Lambaire—after all, perhaps it isn't so bad."

He was slipping back to the old position of second fiddle, his voice betrayed that. Only in his moments of anger did he rise to the domination of his master. In all the years of their association, these strange reversals of mastery had been a feature of their relationship.

Now Lambaire came back to his old position of leader.

"You gas too much, Whitey," he said, as he locked the door and descended the dark stairs. "You take too much for granted, and, moreover, you're a bit too free with your abuse."

"Perhaps I am," said Whitey feebly, "I'm a Jute Factory on Fire when I'm upset."

"I'll be more of a salvage corps in future," said Lambaire humorously.

They dined at a little restaurant in Fleet Street, that being the first they found open in their walk westward.

"All the same," said Whitey, as they sat at dinner, "we've got to get rid of those plates—the note we can explain away; the fact that Amber has it in his possession is more likely to damage him than us —he's a Suspected Person, an' he's under the Act."*

[* Prevention of Crimes Act.]

"That's true," admitted Lambaire, "we'll get rid of them to-morrow; I know a place—¦"

"To-night!" said Whitey definitely. "It's no good waitin' for to-morrow; we might be in the cart to-morrow—we might be in Bridewell to-morrow. I don't like Amber. He's not a policeman, Lambaire—he's a Head—he's got Education and Horse sense—if he gets Funny, we'll be sendin' S.O.S. messages to one another from the cells."

"To-night then," agreed Lambaire hastily; he saw Whitey's anger, so easily aroused, returning to life, "after we've had dinner. And what about Amber—who is he? A swell down on his luck or what?"

Throughout these pages there may be many versions of the rise and fall of Amber, most, indeed all but one, from Amber's lips. Whether Whitey's story was nearer the truth than any other the reader will discover in time.

"Amber? He's Rum. He's been everything, from Cow-boy to Actor. I've heard about him before. He's a Hook because he loves Hooking. That's the long and the short of it. He's been to College."

"College," to Whitey, was a vague and generic term that signified an obscure operation by which learning, of an undreamt-of kind, was introduced to the human mind. College was a place where information was acquired which was not available elsewhere. He had the half educated man's respect for education.

"He got into trouble over a scheme he started for a joke; a sort of you send me-five-shillings-and I'll-do-the-rest. It was so easy that when he came out of gaol he did the same thing with variations He took up hooking just as another chap takes up collecting stamps."

They lingered over their dinner, and the hands of Fleet Street's many clocks were pointing to half-past nine before they had finished.

"We'll walk back," said Lambaire; "it's fortunate that there is no caretaker at Flair Court."

"You've got the key of the outer door?" asked Whitey, and Lambaire nodded.

They passed slowly up Ludgate Hill, arm in arm, two eminently respectable city men, top-hatted, frock-coated, at peace with the world to all outward showing, and perfectly satisfied with themselves.

Flair Court runs parallel with Lothbury, and at this hour of the night is deserted. They passed a solitary policeman, trying the doors of the buildings, and he gave them a civil good night.

Standing at the closed door of the building in which the office was situated, Whitey gave his companion the benefit of his views on the projected Sutton expedition.

"It's our chance, Lambaire," he said, "and the more I think of it the bigger chance it is: why, if it came off we could run straight, there would be money to burn—we could drop the tricky things—forget 'em, Lambaire."

"That's what I thought," said the other, "that was my idea at the time—I was too clever, or I might have brought it off."

He blew at the key.

"What is the matter?" demanded Whitey, suddenly observing his difficulty.

"It's this lock,—I'm not used to the outer door— oh, here we are."

The door-key turned in the lock and the door opened. They closed it behind them, and Lambaire struck a match to light a way up the dark stairs. He lit another at the first landing, and by its light they made their way to the floor above.

Here they stopped.

"Strike a match, Whitey," said Lambaire, and took a key from his pocket.

For some reason the key would not turn.

"That's curious," muttered Lambaire, and brought pressure to bear.

But still the key refused to turn.

Whitey fumbled at the match-box and struck another match.

"Here, let me try," he said.

He pressed the key over, but without success; then he tried the handle of the door.

"It isn't locked," he said, and Lambaire swore.

"It's that cursed fool Grene," he said. "I've told him a thousand times to make certain that he closed and locked the door when he left at night."

He went into the outer office. There was no electric light in the room, and he needed more matches as he made his way to his private room. He took another key and snapped open the patent lock.

"Come in, Whitey," he said, "we'll take these things out of the safe—who's there?"

There was somebody in the room. He felt the presence rather than saw it. The place was in pitch darkness; such light as there was came from a lamp in the Court without, but only the faintest of reflected rays pierced the gloom of the office.

"Keep the door, Whitey," cried Lambaire, and a match spluttered in his hand. For a moment he saw nothing; then, as he peered through the darkness and his eyes became accustomed to the shadows, he uttered an imprecation.

The safe—his private safe, was wide open.

Then he saw the crouching figure of a man by the desk, and leapt at him, dropping the match.

In the expiring flicker of light, he saw the figure straighten, then a fist, as hard as teak, and driven by an arm of steel, caught him full in the face, and he went over with a crash.

Whitey in the doorway sprang forward, but a hand gripped him by the throat, lifted him like a helpless kitten, and sent him with a thud against the wall....

"Strike a match, will you." It was Lambaire who was the first to recover, and he bellowed like a mad bull—" Light—get a light."

With an unsteady hand, Whitey found the box.

"There's a gas bracket over by the window,— curse him!—he's nearly settled me."

The glow of an incandescent lamp revealed Lambaire, dishevelled, pale as death, his face streaming with blood, where he had caught his head on the sharp corner of the desk.

He ran to the safe. There was no apparent disorder, there was no sign that it had been forced; but he turned over the papers, throwing them on to the floor with feverish haste, in his anxiety to find something.

"Gone!" he gasped, "the plates—they've gone!"

He turned, sick with fear, to Whitey.

Whitey was standing, shaky but calm, by the door.

"They've gone, have they?" he said, in little more than a whisper, "then that settles Amber."

"Amber?"

"Amber," said Whitey huskily. "I saw him— you know what it means, don't you?"

"Amber," repeated the other, dazed.

"Amber—*Amber*!" Whitey almost shouted the name. "Don't you hear what I say—it's Amber, the hook."

"What shall we do?"

The big man was like a child in his pitiable terror.

"Do!" Whitey laughed; it was a curious little laugh, and it spoke the concentrated hatred that lay in his heart. "We've got to find Amber, we've got to meet Amber, and we've got to kill Amber, damn him!"

VII. — AMBER GOES TO SCOTLAND YARD

PETER MUSK had the entire top floor of 19, Redcow Court, and was accounted an ideal tenant by his landlord, for he paid his rent regularly. Of the three rooms, Peter occupied one, Amber (" My nephew from the country," said Peter elaborately) the other, and the third was Peter's " common room."

Peter had reached the most exciting chapter in the variegated career of "Handsome Hike, the Terror of Texas," when Amber came in.

He came in hurriedly, and delivered a breathless little chuckle as he closed the door behind him.

Peter looked up over his spectacles, and dropped his romance to his lap. "In trouble?" he demanded eagerly, and when Amber shook his head with a smile, a disappointed frown gathered on the old man's face.

"No, my Peter," said Amber, hanging up his hat, "I am not in trouble—to any extent." He took from his pocket two flat packages and laid them on the table carefully. They were wrapped in newspaper and contained articles of some heavy substance. Amber walked over to the mantel-shelf, where an oil lamp burnt, and examined his coat with minute interest.

"What's up, Amber? What are you looking for?"

"Blood, my Peter," said Amber; "gore—human gore. I was obliged to strike a gentleman hard, with a knobby weapon—to wit, a fist."

"Hey?" Peter was on his feet, all eagerness, but Amber was still smiling.

"Go on with your reading," he said, "there's nothing doin'."

That was a direct and a sharp speech for Amber, and Peter stared, and only the smile saved it from brusqueness.

Amber continued his inspection, removing his coat, and scrutinising the garment carefully.

"No incriminating stains," he reported flippantly, and went to the table, where his packages lay. He had resumed his coat, and, diving into one of the pockets, he produced a flat round leather case. He pressed a spring, and the cover opened like the face of a watch.

Peter was an interested spectator. "That is a compass," he said.

"True, my Peter; it is a compass—but it has the disadvantage that it does not cump: in other words, it is a most unblushing liar of a compass; a misleader of men, my Peter; it is the old one who is the devil of compasses, because it leadeth the feet to stray—in other words it's a dud."

He shook it a little, gave it a twist or two, and shook his head severely. He closed it and put it on the table by his side. Then he turned his attention to the other packages. Very gingerly he unwrapped them. They were revealed as two flat plates of steel, strangely engraved. He leant over them, his smile growing broader and broader, till he broke into a gleeful little laugh.

He looked up to meet the troubled and puzzled eyes of Peter, and laughed out loud.

"Amber, there's a game on," said Peter, gloomily; "there's a dodge on, and I'm not in it. Me that has been with you in every dodge you've worked."

This was not exactly true, but it pleased Peter to believe that he had some part in Amber's many nefarious schemes.

"It's a Dodge and a Game, my Peter," said Amber, carefully wrapping up the plates. "It's this much of a game, that if the police suddenly appeared and found these in my possession I should go down to the tombs for seven long bright years, and you for no less a period."

It may have been an effect of the bad lighting of the room, but it seemed that Peter, the desperate criminal, went a little pale at the prospect so crudely outlined.

"That's a bit dangerous, ain't it?" he said uncomfortably. "Takin' risks of that kind, Amber, —what is it?"

"Forgery," said the calm Amber, "forgery of Bank of England notes."

"Good gaw," gasped Peter, and clutched the edge of the table for support.

"I was thinkin' the same," said Amber, and rose. "I am going to take these precious articles of virtue and bigotry to a safe place," he said.

"Where?—be careful, ol' man—don't get yourself into trouble, an' don't get me into trouble— after me keepin' clear of prison all these years,— chuck 'em into the river; borrer a boat down by Waterloo."

He gave his advice in hoarse whispers as Amber left the room, with a little nod, and continued it over the crazy balustrades, as Amber went lightly down the stairs.

He turned into the Borough, and walked quickly in the direction of London Bridge. He passed a policeman, who, as bad luck would have it, knew him, and the man looked at him hard, then beckoned him.

Amber desired many things, but the one thing in the world that he did not wish was an interview with an inquisitorial policeman. To pass on, pretending not to have noticed the summons, would annoy the man, so Amber stopped, with his most winning smile.

"Well, Mr. Amber," bantered the constable, "I see you're out—going straight now?"

"So straight, my constable," said Amber earnestly, "that you could use my blameless path as a T square." He observed the quick, professional " look over " the man gave him. The plates were showing out of his pocket he knew, and the next remark might easily be a request for information regarding the contents of the flat package. His eye roved for a means of escape, and a slow moving taxicab attracted him. He raised his hand and whistled.

"Doin' the heavy now, are you?" asked the constable disapprovingly.

"In a sense I am," said Amber, and without moving he addressed the chauffeur who had brought his machine to the kerb.

"I want you to take me to New Scotland Yard," he said; then addressing the policeman, he asked, "Do you think Chief Inspector Fell will be on duty?"

"Inspector Fell "—there was a note of respect in the constable's voice—" I couldn't say, we don't know very much about the Yard people—what are you going to see him about?"

"I am afraid I cannot appease your curiosity, my officer," said Amber as he stepped into the cab, "but I will inform the chief inspector that you were anxious to know."

"Here, Amber, none of that! " said the alarmed policeman, stepping to the edge of the pavement, and laying his hand upon the door. "You're not going to say that?"

"Not a bit," Amber grinned, "my little joke; honour amongst policemen, eh?"

The cab made a wide circle, and Amber, looking back through the little back window, saw the policeman standing in that indefinable attitude which expresses doubt and suspicion.

It was a close shave, and Amber breathed a sigh of relief as the danger slipped past. He had ten minutes to decide upon his plan. Being more than ordinary nimble of wit, his scheme was complete before the cab ran smoothly over Westminster Bridge and turned into New Scotland Yard. There was an inspector behind a desk, who looked up from a report he was writing.

"I want to see Mr. Fell," said Amber.

"Name?"

"Amber."

"Seem to know it,—what is the business?"

For answer, Amber laid one hand on the polished counter that separated him from the officer, and placed two fingers diagonally across it.

The inspector grunted affirmatively and reached for the telephone.

"An outside—to see Mr. Fell.... Yes." He hung up the receiver.

"Forty-seven," he said; "you know your way up."

It happened that Amber did not possess this knowledge, but he found no difficulty in discovering number forty-seven, which was a reception-room.

He had a few minutes to wait before a messenger came for him and showed him into a plainly furnished office.

Very little introduction is needed to Josiah Fell, who has figured in every great criminal case during the past twenty years. A short, thick-set man, bald of forehead, with a pointed brown beard. His nose was short and retroussé, his forehead was bald, the flesh about his mild blue eyes was wrinkled and creased by much laughter. He was less like the detective of fiction than the unknowledgable would dare imagine.

"Amber, by heavens!" said the detective. He had a habit of using strong and unnecessary language.

"Amber, my boy, come in and firmey la porte. Well—?"

He unlocked a drawer and produced a box of cigars. He was always glad to meet his "clients," and Amber was an especial favourite of his. Though when he came to think about the matter he had not met Amber professionally.

"You'll have a cigar?"

"What's wrong with 'em?" asked Amber, cautiously selecting one.

"Nothing much," and as Amber lit the cheroot he had taken—" What do you want? Confession, fresh start in life—oh! of course, you've got somebody to put away; they telephoned up that you were doing outside work."

Amber shook his head.

"I told 'em that because I knew that would get me an interview without fuss,—an old convict I met in prison gave me the sign."

He took the packages from his pocket and laid them on the table.

"For me?" queried the officer.

"For you, my Hawkshaw," said Amber.

The detective stripped the paper away, and uttered an exclamation as he saw what the parcels contained.

"Gee—Moses I " He whistled long and softly. "Not your work, Amber? Hardly in your line, eh?"

"Hardly."

"Where did you get them?" Fell looked up quickly as he asked the question.

"That's the one thing I'm not going to tell you," said Amber quietly, "but if you want to know how I got them, I burgled an office and found them in a safe."

"When.?"

"To-night."

The inspector pressed a bell and a policeman came into the room.

"Send an all station message: In the event of an

office burglary being reported, keep the complainant under observation."

The man scribbled the message down and left.

"I send that in case you won't alter your mind about giving me the information I want."

"I'm not likely to tell you," said Amber decisively. "In the first place it won't help you much to know where they came from, unless you can find the factory." The inspector nodded. "When a gang can do work like this, they usually possess more than ordinary resources. If you went for them you'd only bite off a bit of the tail, but the rest of the body would go to earth quicker than money melts."

"I could put them under observation—" began the inspector.

"Pouf! " said Amber scornfully, "pouf, my inspector! Observation be blowed! They'd twig the observer in two shakes; they'd recognise his boots, and his moustache, and his shaven chin. I know your observers. I can pick 'em out in a crowd. No, that's not my idea." Amber hesitated, and appeared to be a little ill at ease.

"Go on, have another cigar, that will help you," encouraged Fell, and opened the box.

"I thank you, but no," said Amber firmly. "I can talk without any such drastic inducement. What I want to say is this;—you know my record?"

"I do," said Fell; "or I think I do, which amounts to the same thing."

"My Chief Inspector," said Amber with some severity, "I beg you to apply your great intellect to a matter which concerns me, as it concerns you. A flippant and a careless interest in the problem I am putting forward, may very well choke the faucet of frankness which at present is turning none too easily. In other words I am embarrassed."

He was silent for awhile; then he got up from the other side of Fell's desk, where he had sat at the detective's invitation, and began to pace the room.

"It's common talk throughout the prisons of England that there is a gang, a real swell gang, putting bank-notes into circulation—not only English but foreign notes," he began.

"It is also common talk in less exclusive circles, Amber, my dear lad," said Fell dryly; "we want that gang badly." He picked up a plate, and held it under the light. "This looks good, but until we 'pull' it I cannot tell how good."

"Suppose "—Amber leant over the table and spoke earnestly—" suppose it is the work of the big gang,—suppose I can track 'em down—"

"Well?"

"Would you find me a billet at the Yard?"

They looked at each other for a space of time, then the lines about the inspector's eyes creased and puckered, and he burst into a roar of laughter.

"My Chief Detective Inspector," said Amber reproachfully, "you hurt me."

But Amber's plaintive protest did not restore the detective's gravity. He laughed until the tears streamed down his face, and Amber watched him keenly.

"Oh dear!" gasped the detective, wiping his eyes. "You're an amusing devil—here." He got up, took a bunch of bright keys from his pocket and opened a cupboard in the wall. From a drawer he took a sheet of foolscap paper, laid it on his desk and sat down.

"Your convictions!" he scoffed.

The paper was ruled exactly down the centre. On the left—to which the detective pointed, were two entries. On the right there was line after line of cramped writing.

"Your imprisonments," said the detective.

Amber said nothing, only he scratched his chin thoughtfully.

"By my reckoning," the detective went on slowly, "you have been sentenced in your short but lurid career to some eighty years' penal servitude."

"It seems a lot," said Amber.

"It does," said the detective, and folded the paper: "So when you come to me and suggest that you would like to turn over a new leaf; would like in fact to join the criminal investigation department, I smile. You've pulled my leg once, but never again. Seriously, Amber," he went on, lowering his voice, "can you do anything for us in this forgery business? —the chief is getting very jumpy about the matter."

Amber nodded.

"I think I can," he said," if I can only keep out of prison for another week."

"Try," said Fell, with a smile.

"I'll try," said Amber cheerfully.

VIII. — FRANCIS SUTTON ASKS A QUESTION

LONDON never sleeps. Of the dead silence that lays over the world, the quiet peaceful hush of all living things, London knows nothing.

Long after the roar of the waking world dies down, there is a fitful rumbling of traffic, a jingling of bells, as belated hansoms come clip-clopping through the deserted streets, the whine of a fast motor-car—then a little silence.

A minute's rest from world noises, then the distant shriek of a locomotive and the staccato clatter of trucks. Somewhere, in a far-away railway yard, with shunters' lanterns swinging, the work of a new day has already begun.

A far-off rattle of slow-moving wheels, nearer and nearer—a market cart on its way to Covent Garden;

a steady tramp of feet—policemen going to their beats in steady procession. More wheels, more shrieks, a church clock strikes the hour, a hurrying footstep in the street....

All these things Lambaire heard, tossing from side to side in his bed. All these and more, for to his ear there came sounds which had no origin save in his imagination. Feet paused at his door; voices whispered excitedly. He heard the click of steel, the squeak of a key opening a handcuff. He dozed at intervals, only to sit up in bed suddenly, the sweat pouring off him, his ears strained to catch some fancied sound. The little clock over the fireplace ticked mercilessly, "ten years, ten years." until he got out of bed, and after a futile attempt to stop it, wrapped it in a towel and then in a dressing-gown to still its ominous prophecy.

All night long he lay, turning over in his mind plans, schemes, methods of escape, if escape were necessary. His bandaged head throbbed unpleasantly, but still he thought, and thought, and thought.

If Amber had the plates, what would he do with them? It was hardly likely he would take them to the police. Blackmail, perhaps. That was more in Amber's line. A weekly income on condition he kept his mouth shut. If that was the course adopted, it was plain sailing. Whitey would do something, Whitey was a desperate, merciless devil.... Lambaire shuddered—there must be no murder though.

He had been reading that very day an article which showed that only four per cent, of murderers in England escape detection... if by a miracle this blew over, he would try a straighter course. Drop the " silver business " and the " printing business " and concentrate on the River of Stars. That was legitimate. If there was anything shady about the flotation of the Company, that would all be forgotten in the splendid culmination.... De Beers would come along and offer to buy a share; he would be a millionaire... other men have made millions and have lived down their shady past. There was Isadore Jarach, who had a palatial residence off Park Lane, he was a bad egg in his beginnings. There was another man... what was his name...?

He fell into a troubled sleep just as the dawn began to show faintly. A knocking at the door aroused him, and he sprang out of bed. He was full of the wildest fears, and his eyes wandered to the desk wherein lay a loaded Derringer.

"Open the door, Lambaire."

It was Whitey's voice, impatiently demanding admission, and with a trembling hand Lambaire slipped back the little bolt of the door.

Whitey entered the room grumbling. If he too had spent a sleepless night, there was little in his appearance to indicate the fact,

"It's a good job you live at an hotel," he said. "I should have knocked and knocked without getting in. Phew! Wreck! You're a wreck."

Whitey shook his head at him disapprovingly.

"Oh, shut up, Whitey!" Lambaire poured out a basin full of water, and plunged his face into it. "I've had a bad night."

"I've had no night at all," said Whitey, "no night at all," he repeated shrilly. "Do I look like a sea-sick turnip? I hope not. You in your little bed,—me, tramping streets looking for Amber—I found him."

Lambaire was wiping his face on a towel, and ceased his rubbing to stare at the speaker.

"You didn't—" he whispered fearfully.

Whitey's lips curled.

"I didn't kill him, if that's what you mean," he said shortly. "Don't jump, Lambaire, you're a great man for jumping—no, I didn't kill him—he lives in the Borough," he added inconsequently.

"How did you find out?" asked Lambaire.

"Don't pad," begged the other testily. "Don't Ask Questions for the sake of Asking Questions,—get dressed,—we'll leave Amber."

"Why?"

Whitey put two long white fingers into his waistcoat pocket and found a golden tooth-pick; he used this absent-mindedly, gazing through the window with a far-away expression.

"Lambaire," he said, as one who speaks to himself, "drop Amber,—cut him out. Concentrate on diamonds."

"That's what I thought," said Lambaire eagerly, "perhaps if we went out ourselves and looked round—"

"Go out be—blowed," snapped Whitey. "If you see me going out to Central Africa... heat... fever... Rot! No, we'll see the young lady, tell her the tale; throw ourselves, in a manner of speaking, on her mercy—I've fixed an interview with young Sutton."

"Already?"

"Already," said Whitey. "Got him on the 'phone."

"What about Amber and the plates?"

"Blackmail," said Whitey, and Lambaire chuckled gleefully.

"So I thought, of course that is the idea—what about Sutton?"

"He's coming here to breakfast; hurry up with your dressing."

Half-an-hour later Lambaire joined him in the big lounge of the hotel. A bath and a visit to the hotel barber had smartened him, but the traces of his night with Conscience had not been entirely removed, and the black silk bandage about his head gave him an unusually sinister appearance.

On the stroke of nine came Francis Sutton, carrying himself a little importantly, as became an explorer *in embryo*, and the three adjourned to the dining-room.

There is a type of character which resolutely refuses to be drawn, and Francis Sutton's was such an one. It was a character so elusive, so indefinite, so exasperatingly plastic, that the outline one might draw to-day would be false to-morrow. Much easier would it be to sketch a nebula, or to convey in the medium of black and white the changing shape of smoke, than to give verity to this amorphous soul.

The exact division of good and bad in him made him vague enough; for no man is distinguished unless there is an overbalancing of qualities. The scale must go down on the one side or the other, or, if the adjustment of virtue and evil is so nice that the scale's needle trembles hesitatingly between the two, be sure that the soul in the balance is colourless, formless, vague.

Francis Sutton possessed a responsive will, which took inspiration from the colour and temperature of the moment. He might start forth from his home charged with a determination to act in a certain direction, and return to his home in an hour or so, equally determined, but in a diametrically opposite course, and, curiously enough, be unaware of any change in his plans.

Once he had come to Lambaire for an interview which was to be final. An interview which should thrust out of his life an unpleasant recollection (he usually found this process an easy one), and should establish an independence of which—so he deluded himself—he was extremely jealous. On this occasion he arrived in another mood; he came as the approved protégé of a generous patron.

"Now we've got to settle up matters," said Lambaire as they sat at breakfast. "The impertinence of that rascally friend of yours completely put the matter out of my mind yesterday—"

"I'm awfully sorry about that business," Sutton hastened to say. "It is just like Cynthia to get mixed up with a scoundrel like Amber. I assure you—"

Lambaire waved away the eager protestations with a large smile.

"My boy," he said generously, "say no more about it. I exonerate you from all blame, don't I, Whitey?"

Whitey nodded with vigour.

"I know Amber"—Lambaire tapped his bandaged head—"this is Amber."

"Good lord!" said the boy with wide-opened eyes, "you don't mean that?"

"I do," said the other. "Last night, coming back to the hotel, I was set upon by Amber and half a dozen roughs—wasn't I, Whitey?"

"You was," said White, who at times rose superior to grammatical conventions.

"But the police?" protested the young man energetically. "Surely you could lay him by the heels?"

Lambaire shook his head with a pained smile.

"The police are no good," he said, "they're all in the swim together—my dear boy, you've no idea of the corruption of the police force; I could tell you stories that would raise your hair."

He discoursed at some length on the iniquities of the constabulary.

"Now let us get to business," he said, passing back his plate. "Have you thought over my suggestion?"

"I've given the matter a great deal of thought," said Sutton. "I suppose there will be a contract and all that sort of thing?"

"Oh, certainly,—I'm glad you asked. We were talking about that very thing this morning, weren't we, Whitey?"

Whitey nodded, and yawned furtively. "I'm afraid your sister is prejudiced against us," Lambaire went on. "I regret this: it pains me a little. She is under the impression that we want to obtain possession of the plan she has. Nothing of the sort I We do not wish to see the plan. So far as we know, the river lies due north west through the Alebi country. As a matter of fact," said Lambaire in confidence, "we don't expect that plan to be of very much use to you, do we, Whitey?"

"Yes," said Whitey absently—" no, I mean."

"Our scheme is to send you out and give you an opportunity of verifying the route."

They spoke in this strain for the greater part of an hour, discussing equipment and costs, and the boy, transported on the breath of fancy to another life and another sphere, talked volubly, being almost incoherent in his delight.

But still there were the objections of Cynthia Sutton to overcome.

"A matter of little difficulty," said the boy airily, and the two men did not urge the point, knowing that, so far from being a pebble on the path, to be lightly brushed aside, this girl, with her clear vision and sane judgment, was a very rock.

Later in the morning, when they approached the house in Warwick Gardens, they did not share the assurance of the chattering young man who led the way.

Francis Sutton had pressed the knob of the electric bell, when he turned suddenly to the two men.

"By the way," he said, "whose mine was this? —yours or my father's?"

The naiveté of the question took Lambaire off his guard.

"Your father discovered it," he said, unthinkingly, and as he stopped, Whitey came to his rescue.

"But we floated it," he said, in a tone that suggested that on the score of ownership no more need be said.

IX. — AMBER SEES THE MAP

CYNTHIA SUTTON was twenty-three, and, by all standards, beautiful. Her hair was a rich chestnut, her eyes were big, and of that shade which is either blue or grey, according to the light in which they were seen. Her nose was straight, her upper lip short; her lips full and red, her skin soft and unblemished. "She has the figure of a woman, and the eyes of a child," said Amber describing her " and she asked me to come to tea."

"And you didn't go," said Peter, nodding his head approvingly. "You realized that your presence might compromise this innercent flower. 'No,' you sez to yourself, 'no, I will go away, carrying a fragrant memory, an'—'"

"To be exact, my Peter," said Amber, "I forgot all about the appointment in the hurry and bustle of keeping out of Lambaire's way."

They were sitting in the little room under the roof of 19, Redcow Court, and the sweet song of the caged birds filled the apartment with liquid melody.

"No," continued Amber thoughtfully, "I must confess to you, my Peter, that I had none of those interestin' conversations with myself that your romantic soul suggests."

He looked at his watch. It was ten o'clock in the forenoon, and he stared through the open window, his mind intent upon a problem.

"I ought to see her," he said, half to himself; he was groping for excuses. "This business of young Sutton's... compass and chart... hidden treasures and all that sort of thing, eh, my Peter?"

Peter's eyes were gleaming from behind his gold-rimmed spectacles, and his hand shook with excitement, as he rose and made his way to the cretonne- curtained shelves.

"I've got a yarn here," he said, fumbling eagerly amongst his literary treasures, "that will give you some ideas: money and pieces of eight—what is a piece of eight?" He turned abruptly with the question.

"A sovereign," said Amber promptly, "eight half-crowns." He was in the mood when he said just the first thing that came into his head.

"Um!" Peter resumed his search, and Amber watched him with the gentle amusement that one reserves for the enthusiasm of children at play.

"Here it is," said Peter.

He drew forth from a pile of books one, gaudy of colour and reckless of design. "This is the thing,"— he dusted the paper cover tenderly—" 'Black Eyed Nick, or the Desperado's Dream of Ducats'; how's that?"

Amber took the book from the old man and inspected it, letting the pages run through his fingers rapidly.

"Fine," he said, with conviction. "Put it with my pyjamas, I'll read myself to sleep with it "— he spoke a little absently, for his mind was elsewhere.

It was a relief to him when Peter left him to "shop." Shopping was the one joy of Peter's life, and usually entailed a very careful rehearsal.

"A penn'oth of canary seed, a quarter of tea, two of sugar, four bundles of wood, a pint of paraffin, tell the greengrocer to send me half a hundred of coal, eggs, bit of bacon—you didn't like the bacon this morning, did you, Amber?—some kippers, a chop—how will a chop suit you?—and a pound of new potatoes; I think that's all."

Leaning out of the window, Amber saw him disappearing up the court, his big rush bag gripped tightly in his hand, his aged top-hat tilted to the back of his head.

Amber waited until he was out of sight, then made his way to his bedroom and commenced to change his clothes.

A quarter of an hour later he was on his way to Warwick Gardens.

The maid who answered his knock told him that her mistress was engaged, but showed him into a little study.

"Take her a note," said Amber, and scribbled a message in his pocket book, tearing out the leaf.

When the twisted slip of paper came to her, Cynthia was engaged in a fruitless and so far as Lambaire was concerned, a profitless discussion on her brother's projected expedition. She opened the note and coloured. "Yes," she said with a nod to the maid, and crumpled the note in her hand.

"I hardly think it is worth while continuing this discussion," she said; "it is not a question of my approval or disapproval: if my brother elects to take the risk, he will go whatever my opinions are on the subject."

"But, my dear young lady," said Lambaire eagerly, "you are wrong; it isn't only the chart which you have placed at our disposal—"

"At my brother's," she corrected.

"It isn't only that," he went on, "it's the knowledge that you are in sympathy with our great project: it means a lot to us, ye know, Miss Cynthia—"

"Miss Sutton," she corrected again.

"It means more than you can imagine; I've made a clean breast of my position. On the strength of your father's statement about this mine, I floated a company; I spent a lot of money on the expedition. I sent him out to Africa with one of the best caravans that have been got together—and now the shareholders are bothering me. 'Where's that mine of yours?' they say. Why "—his voice sank to an impressive whisper—" they talk of prosecuting me, don't they, Whitey?"

"They do indeed," said his responsive companion truthfully.

"So it was a case of fair means or foul," he went on. "I had to get the plan, and you wouldn't give it me. I couldn't burgle your house for it, could I?"

He smiled pleasantly at the absurdity of taking such a course, and she looked at him curiously.

"It is strange that you should say that," she replied slowly, "for remarkably enough this house was burgled twice after my refusal to part with the little map."

"Remarkable!" said Lambaire.

"Astoundin'!" said Whitey, no less surprised.

She rose from her chair.

"Since the matter has been settled—so far as I have anything to do with it," she said, "you will excuse my presence."

She left the room, and Amber, sitting in the little study, heard the swish of her skirts and rose to meet her.

There was a touch of pink in her cheeks, but she was very grave and self- possessed, as she favoured him with the slightest of bows and motioned him to a seat.

"Good of you to see me, Miss Sutton," said Amber.

She noted, with a little pang, that he was quite at ease. There could be little hope for a man who was so lost to shame that he gloried in his misspent career rather than showed some indication of embarrassment in the presence of a woman who knew him for what he was.

"I felt I owed you this interview at least," she replied steadily. "I wish—" She stopped.

"Yes?" Amber perked his head on one side inquiringly, "You were going to say that you wished—?"

"It does not matter," she said. She felt herself blushing.

"You wish you could do something for me," he said with a half-smile, "but, my lady, half the good people in the world are trying to do something for me. I am hopeless, I am incorrigible; regard me as that."

Nevertheless, lightly as he discussed the question of his regeneration, he eyed her keenly to see how she would take the rejection of help. To his relief, and somewhat to his annoyance also, be it admitted, he observed she accepted his valuation of himself very readily.

"I have come to see you to-day," he went on, "in relation to a matter which is of supreme importance to you. Do you mind answering a few questions I put to you?"

"I have no objection," she said. "Your father was an explorer, was he not?"

"Yes."

"He knew Central Africa very well?" " Yes,—very well."

"He discovered a mine—a diamond mine, or something of the sort?"

She shook her head with a smile.

"That has yet to be proved," she said. "He had heard, from the natives, of a wonderful river—the River of Stars they called it, because in its bed were stones, many of which had been polished by the action of the water until they glittered,—they were undoubtedly diamonds, for my father purchased a number from the people of the country."

Amber nodded.

"And then I suppose he came home and got into touch with Lambaire?"

"That is so," she said, wondering at the course the interview was taking.

Amber nodded thoughtfully.

"The rest of the story I know," he said. "I was at pains to look up the circumstances attending your father's death. You received from the Commissioner of the district a chart?"

She hesitated.

"I did—yes."

He smiled.

"I have no designs upon the mine, but I am anxious to see the chart—and before you refuse me, Miss Sutton, let me tell you that I am not prompted by idle curiosity."

"I believe that, Mr. Amber," she said; "if you wait, I will get it for you."

She was gone for ten minutes and returned with a long envelope. From this she extracted a soiled sheet of paper and handed it to the ex-convict.

He took it, and carried it to the window, examining it carefully.

"I see the route is marked from a point called Chengli—where is that?"

"In the Alebi forest," she said; "the country is known as far as Chengli; from there on, my father mapped the country, inquiring his way from such natives as he met—this was the plan he had set himself."

"I see."

He looked again at the map, then from his pocket he took the compass he had found in Lambaire's safe. He laid it on the table by the side of the map and produced a second compass, and placed the two instruments side by side.

"Do you observe any difference in these, Miss Sutton?" he asked, and the girl looked carefully.

"One is a needle compass, and on the other there is no needle," she said.

"That is so; the whole of the dial turns," Amber nodded. "Nothing else?" he asked.

"I can see no other difference," she said, shaking her head.

"Where is the north on the dial?"

She followed the direction of the letter N and pointed.

"Where is the north of the needle?"

Her brows knit in a puzzled frown, for the thin delicate needle of the smaller compass pointed never so slightly in a more westerly direction than its fellow.

"What does that mean?" she asked, and their eyes met over the table.

Lambaire and his host had finished their business. Francis Sutton was in a jubilant mood, and came into the hall with his patron.

"You mustn't worry about my sister," he said; "she'll come round to my way of thinking after a while—she's a woman, you know," he added, vaguely.

"I understand, my boy," said the expansive Lambaire. "We both understand, don't we, Whitey?"

"Certainly," said Whitey.

"Still, she'll probably be annoyed if you go off without saying good-bye,—where is your mistress

Susan?" he asked of the maid who had come in answer to his bell.

"In the study, sir."

"Come along." He led the way to the study and opened the door.

"Cynthia—" he began.

They were leaning over the table; between them lay the map and the two compasses. What Sutton saw, the other two saw; and Lambaire, sweeping past the youth, snatched up his property.

"So that's the game, is it?" he hissed: he was trembling with passion; "that's your little game, Amber !"

He felt Whitey's hand grip his arm and recovered a little of his self-possession.

"This man is not content with attempting to blackmail," he said, "not content with committing a burglary at my office and stealing valuable drawings—"

"What does this mean, Cynthia?"

Sutton's voice was stern, and his face was white with anger. For the second time Amber came to the rescue. "Allow me," he said.

"I'll allow you nothing," stormed the boy; "get out of this house before I kick you out. I want no gaol birds here,"

"It is a matter of taste, my Francis," said the imperturbable Amber; "if you stand Lambaire you'd stand anybody."

"I'll settle with you later," said Lambaire darkly.

"Settle now," said Amber in his most affable manner. "Mr. Sutton," he said, "that man killed your father, and he will kill you."

"I want none of your lies," said Sutton; "there's the door."

"And a jolly nice door too," said Amber; "but I didn't come here to admire your fixtures: ask Lambaire to show you the compass, or one like it, that he provided for your father's expedition. Send it to Greenwich and ask the astronomers to tell you how many points it is out of the true—they will work out to a mile or so how far wrong a man may go who made his way by it, and tried to find his way back from the bush by short cuts."

"Francis, you hear this?" said the girl.

"Rubbish!" replied the youth contemptuously, "what object could Mr. Lambaire have had? He didn't spend thousands of pounds to lose my father in the bush! The story isn't even plausible, for, unless my father got back again to civilization with the plan, the expedition was a failure."

"Exactly!" applauded Lambaire, and smiled triumphantly.

Amber answered smile for smile.

"It wasn't the question of his getting back, as I understand the matter," he said quietly, "it was a question whether, having located the mine, and having returned with the map, and the compass, whether anybody else would be able to locate it, or find their way to it, without Lambaire's Patent Compass."

The tangled skein of the plot was unravelled before the girl's eyes, and she looked from Amber to the stout Lambaire.

"I see, I see," she whispered. "Francis," she cried, "don't you understand what it all means?"

"I understand that you're a fool," he said roughly; "if you've finished your lies, you can go, Amber."

"I have only a word to add,"—Amber picked up his hat. "If you do not realize that Lambaire is the biggest wrong 'un outside prison—I might add for your information that he is a notorious member of the Big Five Gang; a forger of bank notes and Continental securities; he has also a large interest in a Spanish coining establishment— didn't^think I knew it, eh, my Lambie?—where real silver half-crowns are manufactured at a profit, thanks to the fact that silver is a drug on the market. Beyond that I know nothing against him."

"There's the door," said Sutton again.

"Your conversation is decidedly monotonous," said Amber, and with a smile and a friendly nod to the girl, he left.

X. — THE MAN IN CONVICT'S CLOTHES

ALPHONSE LAMBAIRE was a man of many interests.

In his forty-two years of life he had collected them as another man might collect old prints. That he started forth at the outset, and of perversity chose the shadier walks of life, is a supposition which need not seriously be entertained, for it is not in accordance with the rule of things that a man should deliberately set himself in opposition to the laws of civilization.

All that Amber had said of him was true, and more.

He was a coiner in the sense that, with the notorious Señor Villitissi, and the no less notorious companions of that sometime senator, he had to do with the alarming increase in the silver coinage from which the markets of the world suffered.

It is a known fact that one "batch" of coins which was distributed in Spain, brought the rate of exchange from twenty-eight pesetas ten to thirty-one pesetas in a month.

There was nothing about him which suggested the strutting villain of melodrama, yet he was a well-defined type of criminal.

Whitey—Cornelius Josiah White, to give him the only name which ever appeared to have a resemblance to a real name employed by him—was a lesser man in point of originality, greater when measured by the standards of daring and crude villainy.

Whitey said as much one afternoon, about a week after the interview.

"What you want, Lambaire, is Dash," he said. "When the least little bit of trouble comes along, instead of Swelling up to it, you get Shrunk."

Lambaire grunted something.

He was in no mood for psychology.

They were on their way to Warwick Gardens for a final interview with Sutton and his sister.

"After Amber's 'give away,'" Whitey went on, "you'd have chucked the whole business; you would, Lambaire! You'd have chucked it for a hook like Amber... your big schemes too, Imperial I call 'em... along comes a feller fresh from gaol, a swell thief, and you start looking round for Exits-in-case-of- Emergency."

"I was afraid Sutton would turn me down."

"Bosh!" said Whitey unsympathetically, "he couldn't turn you down without turning down himself: don't you know that chaps of his age will do anything to prove they are right?"

"Well the girl isn't convinced," objected Lambaire.

"And never will be," said Whitey, "you're the Devil to her," Lambaire's face went unaccountably black at this frank expression, and Whitey, who had forgotten more about human nature than Lambaire was ever likely to learn, was wise enough to leave the subject unpursued.

They were admitted to the house and ushered into Sutton's room.

The youth sat amidst a litter of catalogues, maps, and samples of equipment. He was sitting in his shirt sleeves, smoking a pipe, and was obviously and most absurdly pleased with himself.

He greeted his visitors with a cheerful smile.

"Come in, and find a place to sit down if you can," he invited. "I will let Cynthia know that you are here." He leant back and pushed a bell by the side of the fireplace.

" We had better fix up the question of the chart," he said; "that confounded man Amber has upset everything; you know how suspicious women are, and the dear girl suspects you good people of all sorts of sinister plans."

He laughed heartily at the joke of it.

A servant appeared at the door and he sent a message to his sister.

"I have succeeded in persuading her," he went on, "to let me have the chart."

Lambaire breathed an inward sigh of relief, and the twinkling eyes of Whitey danced with glee.

"It will surprise you to learn that, save for a momentary glimpse, even I have never seen it," he said, "and really, after all the bother that has been made about the thing, I shall be disappointed if it is not the most lucid of documents."

Cynthia Sutton came into the room at that moment.

She favoured Lambaire with a distant bow, and ignored the extravagant politeness of Whitey, who was the only one of the party that stood.

Lambaire, with an eye for the beautiful, and having for the first time leisure to observe her, noted with a pleasant feeling of surprise that she was more than ordinarily pretty. Her features were perfectly modelled, her eyes were large and grey, she was slender and tall, and her every movement betrayed her supple grace.

For the first time, Lambaire viewed her as a woman, and not as an antagonist, and he enjoyed the experience.

She stood by the table where her brother sat, her hands behind her, looking down at him gravely.

Whitey derived no small amount of satisfaction from the fact that from where he sat he saw that in one hand she held an envelope of a large size. He guessed that therein was the chart which had been the subject of so much discussion.

This proved to be the case, for without preamble, she produced two sheets of paper. The first was a discoloured and stained little map, drawn on thick cartridge paper.

It was blistered by heat, and bore indications of rough treatment. The second sheet was clean, and this she placed before her brother.

He looked at it wonderingly, then raised his eyes to the girl's face with a puzzled air.

"Yes," she said, as in answer to his unspoken question, "this is a copy, but I have brought the original that you may compare it." She laid the discoloured plan by its side. "The copy is a perfect one," she said.

"But why on earth do you want a copy?"

For answer she slipped the original into the envelope again.

"The copy is for you," she said, "the original I shall keep."

Sutton was too pleased to secure the plan to care overmuch whether it was the original or a copy As he pored over it insensibly the two men were drawn to the table.

"It is a rum-looking map—my father seems to have gone in a half-circle."

"What I can't understand is this dotted line," said the youth, and indicated a straight line that formed the base of an obtuse triangle, the other two sides being formed by the travellers' route.

"I think this is a favourable moment to make an explanation," said Lambaire in his gentlest voice. He addressed himself to the girl, who shifted her gaze from her brother's face to his.

"On the occasion of my last visit here," he continued, "there was a painful scene, which was not of my seeking. A man I can only describe as a—a—"

"Dangerous bloke—fellow," said Whitey, correcting himself in some confusion.

"A dangerous fellow," repeated Lambaire, "who made wild and reckless charges against my honesty. That man, who has been an inmate of every gaol—"

"I do not think you need go into particulars of Mr. Amber's career."

There was the faintest touch of pink in her cheeks as she changed the course of Lambaire's speech.

"As you wish." He was irritated, for he was a man of no very great gift of speech, and he had come prepared with his explanation. "I only wish to say this, that the man Amber spoke the truth— though his—"

"Deductions?" suggested Whitey *sotto voce*.

"Though his deductions were wrong: the compass your father used was a faulty one."

The girl's eyes did not leave his face.

"It was a faulty one," continued Lambaire, "and it was only yesterday that I discovered the fact. There were four compasses made, two of which your father had, and two I kept locked up in my safe."

"Why was that?" questioned the girl.

"That is easily explained," responded the other eagerly. "I knew that even if Mr. Sutton succeeded, another expedition would be necessary, and as a business man, I of course bought in a business like manner—one buys these instruments cheaper—"

"By taking a quantity," murmured Whitey.

"In a sense," continued Lambaire impressively, "that precaution of mine has made this expedition of your brother's possible. We are now able to follow in your father's track—for we shall work by the compass he used."

He felt that his explanation was all that was necessary. More than this, he half-believed all that he had said, and felt an inexplicable sense of satisfaction in the realization of his forethought.

Cynthia said nothing. She had gone beyond the place where she felt the duty or inclination to oppose her brother's will. It could be said with truth that her brother and his project had faded into the background, for there had come a newer and a more astounding interest into her life.

She did not confess as much to herself. It was the worst kind of madness.

A convict—with not even the romantic interest of a great conviction. A mean larcenist, for all the polish of his address, and the gay humour of those honest eyes of his.

Her brother would go to the coast in search of the River of Stars. Possibly he might find it: she was sufficiently blessed with the goods of this world not to care whether he did or not. She would like her father's judgment vindicated, but here again she had no fervency of desire to that end.

Her father had been a vague shadow of a man, with little or no concern with his family. His children, during the rare periods he stayed in the same house with them, had been " noises " to be incontinently " stopped."

All her love had been lavished on her brother, her struggles, in the days before the happy legacy had placed her beyond the need for struggling, had been for his comfort and ease. She had been willingly blind to his follies, yet had been frantic in her efforts to check those follies from degenerating into vices... She remembered she had been on the verge of tears the first time she met Amber, and almost smiled at the recollection.

Francis would go out, and would come back again alive: she had no doubt about this: the tiny ache in her heart had an origin foreign to the question of her brother's safety.

All this passed through her mind, as she stood by the table pretending to listen to a conversation which had become general.

She became alert when Lambaire returned to a forbidden subject.

"I don't know why he has interfered," he was saying, answering a question Sutton had addressed to him; "that night he came into the Whistlers—"

A warning caught from Whitey brought him on to another tack. "Well, well," he said benevolently, "it is not for us to judge the poor fellow, one doesn't know what temptations assail a man: he probably saw an opportunity for making easy money," another cough from Whitey, and he pulled out his watch. "I must be getting along," he said, "I have to meet a man at Paddington: would you care to come? I have one or two other matters to talk over with you." Sutton accepted the invitation with alacrity. What impelled Cynthia Sutton to take the step she did it is difficult to say. It may have been the merest piece of feminine curiosity, a mischievous desire to hinder the free exchange of ideas; the chances are that another explanation might be found, for as Sutton left the room to change his coat she turned to Lambaire and asked— " What is Mr. Amber's history?" Lambaire smiled and glanced significantly at Whitey.

"Not a very nice one, eh, Whitey?" Whitey shook his head.

"I am a little interested," she said; "should I be a bother to you if I walked with you to Paddington— it is a beautiful afternoon."

"Madam," said the gratified Lambaire, "I shall be overjoyed. I feel that if I can only gain your confidence—I was saying this morning, wasn't I, Whitey?"

"You were," said the other instantly. "I was saying, 'Now if I could only get Miss Cynthia—'"

"Miss Sutton," said Cynthia.

"I beg your pardon, Miss Sutton, to see my point of view..."

"I won't promise that," she said with a smile, as her brother returned.

He was inclined to be annoyed when she walked ahead with his patron, but his annoyance was certainly not shared by Lambaire, who trod on air.

"...Yes, I'm afraid Amber is a bad egg—a wrong 'un, ye know. He's not Big."

Her heart sank as she recognized the echo of her own thoughts. It was absurd that the mediocrity of Amber's criminal attainments should fill her with numb despair, but so it was.

"No, he's not Big—although," said Lambaire hastily, "I've no sympathy for the Big Mob."

"With the—?"

She was puzzled.

"With the Big Mob—the high-class nuts—you know what I mean—the—" He looked round helplessly for Whitey.

"I think I understand," she said.

They walked on in silence for another five minutes.

"Do you think that if some good influence were brought to bear on a man like Mr. Amber—"

"No, absolutely no, miss," said Lambaire emphatically, "he's the sort of man that only gaol can reform. A friend of mine, who is Governor of Clemstead Gaol, told me that Amber was one of the most hardened prisoners he'd ever had—there's no hope for a man like that."

Cynthia sighed. In a vague way she wondered how it came about that such a man as she judged Lambaire to be, should have friends in the prison service.

"A bad lot," said Lambaire as they turned into the station.

On the platform Cynthia took her brother aside, whilst the other two were making inquiries regarding the arrival of a train.

"I shall go back to the house—I suppose you are determined to go through with this expedition?"

"Of course," irritably; "for Heaven's sake, Cynthia, don't let us go into this matter again."

She shrugged her shoulders, and was about to make some remark, when Lambaire came hurrying along the platform, his face eloquent of triumph.

"Look here," he said, and beckoned.

Wondering what could have animated this lymphatic man, she followed with her brother.

She turned a corner of the station building, then came to a sudden stop, and went white to the lips.

Under the care of two armed warders were a dozen convicts in the ugly livery of their servitude.

They were chained wrist to wrist, and each handcuff was fastened to the next by a steel chain.

Conspicuous in the foremost file was Amber, bright, cheerful, unaffected by this ignominious situation.

Then he saw the girl, and his eyes dropped and a scarlet flush came to his tanned cheek.

"My Lambaire," he murmured, "I owe you one for this."

XI. — INTRODUCES CAPTAIN AMBROSE GREY

"YOU'RE for the governor, 634," said the warder.

"You surprise me, my warder," said Amber ironically.

"Less of your lip," said the man shortly, "you've lost enough marks in this month without askin' for any further trouble."

Amber said nothing. He stepped out from his cell and marched ahead of the warder down the steel stairway that led to the ground floor of the prison hall.

Captain Cardeen sat behind his table and greeted Amber unpleasantly.

Exactly why he should take so vindictive an interest in his charge, could be explained.

"634," said the governor, "you've been reported

again for impertinence to an officer of the prison."

Amber made no reply.

"Because you spend half your life in prison I suppose you've an idea that you've got a sort of proprietorial right, eh?"

Still Amber made no reply.

"I have tamed a few men in my time," the governor went on, "and I don't doubt but that I shall tame you."

Amber was looking at him critically.

"Sir," said he, "I also am something of a tamer."

The governor's face went purple, for there was an indefinable insolence in the prisoner's tone.

"You scoundrel," he began, but Amber interrupted him.

"I am tired of prison life, my governor," he said brusquely, "and I'll take a thousand to thirty you do not know what I mean: I am tired of this prison, which is Hell with the lid off."

"Take him back to his cell," roared the governor, on his feet and incoherent with rage. "I'll teach you, my man—I'll have you flogged before I'm through with you."

Two warders, truncheons in hand, hustled Amber through the door. They flung rather than pushed him into the cell. A quarter of an hour later a key turned in the door and two warders came in, the foremost dangling a pair of bright steel handcuffs.

Amber was prepared: he turned about obediently as they snapped the irons about his wrist, fastening his hands behind him. It was a favourite punishment of Captain Cardeen.

The door clanged to, and he was left alone with his thoughts, and for Amber, remembering his equable temperament, they were very unpleasant thoughts indeed.

"I'll teach him something," said the governor to his chief warder. "I know something about this man—I had a letter some time ago from a fellow- member of the Whistlers—one of my clubs, Mr. Rice —who gave me his history."

"If anybody can break him, you can, sir," said his admiring satellite.

"I think so," said the governor complacently.

A warder interrupted any further exchange of views. He handed a letter to the chief warder with a salute, and that official glanced at the address and passed it on to his superior.

The latter slipped his finger through the flap of the envelope and opened it.

The sheet of blue foolscap it contained required a great deal of understanding, for he read it three times.

```
"The bearer of this, Miss Cynthia Sutton, has permission to
interview No. 634 /c.c./ John Amber. The interview shall be a
private one: no warder is to be present."
```

It was signed with the neat signature of the Home Secretary and bore the Home Office stamp.

The governor looked up with bewilderment written in his face.

"What on earth is the meaning of that?" he demanded, and passed the paper to the chief warder.

The latter read it and pushed back his head.

"It's against all regulations—" he began, but the governor broke in impatiently.

"Don't talk nonsense about regulations," he snapped. "Here is an order from the Home Office: you can't get behind that. Is anybody with her?"

He addressed the question to the waiting warder.

"Yes, sir, a gentleman from Scotland Yard—I gave you his card."

The card had fallen on to the floor and the governor picked it up.

"Chief Inspector Fells," he read, "let us have him in first."

A few seconds later Fells came into the room, and smiled a cheerful greeting to the governor.

"Perhaps you can explain the meaning of this, Mr. Fells," said the governor, holding the paper in his hand.

Fells shook his head.

"I never explain anything," he said. "It's the worst waste of energy to attempt to explain the actions of your superiors—I've got an order too."

"To see the prisoner?"

"Yes, sir."

He groped in the depths of an under pocket and produced an official envelope.

"I have spoken to the young lady," he said, "and she has no objection to my seeing Mr. Amber first."

There was something about that " Mr." which annoyed the governor.

"I can understand many things," he said irritably, "but I really cannot understand the process of mind which induces you to refer to a convict as 'Mr. Amber'—a man with your experience of criminals, Inspector."

"Habit, sir, habit," said Fells easily, "a slip of the tongue."

The governor was reading the new order, which was couched in similar terms to that which he had already read.

"You had better see him first," and made a sign to the chief warder. "The beggar has been grossly impertinent and is now undergoing a little mild punishment."

"M—m—yes," hesitated the detective; "pardon my asking, but isn't this the goal where the man Gallers died?"

"It is," said the governor coldly; "he had a fit or a something."

"He was undergoing some punishment," said Fells, in the reflective tone of one striving to recollect a circumstance.

"It was stated so by irresponsible people," said the governor roughly.

He took down his hat from a peg and put it on. "It was said he was being punished in the same manner that Amber is—that he became ill and was unable to ring the bell—but it was a lie."

"Of course," said the polite detective.

The governor led the way through the spotless corridors up the steel stairs to the landing whereon Amber's cell was situated. He turned the key and entered, followed by the detective. Amber was sitting on a wooden stool when the cell door opened.

He did not trouble to rise until he saw Fells. Then he got up with difficulty.

"Now, Mr. Fells, if you have anything to say to this man, you had better say it," said the governor.

"I think," Fells spoke hesitatingly, deferentially, but none the less emphatically, "I think I may have this interview alone—yes?"

The governor stiffened.

"If you would prefer it, of course," he said grudgingly, and turned to go.

"Excuse me," Fells laid his hand on the official's arm. "I would rather the irons were off this man."

"Attend to your business and allow me to attend to mine, Mr. Inspector," said the governor. "The code allows me the right to award punishment."

"Very good, sir," replied Fells. He waited until the door clanged and then turned to Amber.

"Mr. Amber," he said, "I have been sent down from the Home Office on a curious mission—I understand you are tired of prison?"

"My Fells," said Amber wearily, "I have never found prison so dull as I do at present."

Fells smiled. From his pocket he produced a sheet of foolscap paper closely covered with entries.

"I've discovered your guilty secret." He shook the paper before the prisoner's eyes. "A list of your convictions, my Amber," he mocked, but Amber said nothing.

"Never, so far as I can trace, have you appeared before a judge and jury." He looked up, but the man in front of him was silent, and his face was expressionless.

"And yet," the detective went on, "to my knowledge, you have been committed to seventeen gaols, on seventeen distinct and separate orders, each signed by a judge and counter-signed by the Home Office..."

He waited, but Amber offered no comment.

"In 1901, you were committed to Chengford Gaol on an order signed at Devizes. I can find no record of your having been brought before a court of any description at Devizes."

Still Amber did not speak, and the inspector went on slowly and deliberately.

"At the time of your committal to Chengford, there had been all sorts of stories current about the state of affairs in the gaol. There had been a mutiny of prisoners, and allegations of cruelty against the governor and the warders.

"I remember something about it," said Amber carelessly.

"You were admitted on May 10. On August

I you were released on an order from the Home Office. On August 3 the governor, the assistant governor and the chief warder were summarily suspended from their duties and were eventually dismissed from the prison service."

He looked at Amber again.

"You surprise me," said Amber.

"Although you were released in August, and was apparently a free man, you arrived in the custody of warders at the Preston Convict Establishment on September 9. There had been some trouble at Preston, I believe."

"I believe there was," said Amber gravely.

"This time," the detective continued, "it was on an order from the Home Office 'to complete sentence.' You were six months in Preston Prison, and after you left, three warders were suspended for carrying messages to prisoners."

He ran his fingers down the paper.

"You weren't exactly a mascot to these gaols, Mr. Amber," he said ironically, "you left behind you a trail of casualties—and nobody seems to have connected your presence with gaps in the ranks."

A slow smile dawned on Amber's face.

"And has my chief inspector come amblin' all the way from London to make these startlin' and mysterious communications?"

The detective dropped his banter.

"Not exactly, Mr. Amber," he said, and the note of respect came to his voice which had so unaccountably irritated the governor. "The fact is, you've been lent."

"Lent?" Amber's eyebrows rose.

"You've been lent," repeated the detective. "The Home Office has lent you to the Colonial Office, and I am here to effect the transfer."

Amber twiddled his manacled hands restlessly.

"I don't want to go out of England just now," he began.

"Oh yes, you do, Mr. Amber, there's a River of Stars somewhere in the world, and a cargo of roguery on its way to locate it."

"So they've gone, have they?"

He was disappointed and did not attempt to disguise the fact.

"I hoped that I should be out in time to stop 'em, but that racket has nothing to do with the Colonial Office."

"Hasn't it?"

Fells went to the wall where the prisoner's bell was, and pushed it. Two minutes later the door swung open.

"There's another visitor, who will explain," he said, and left the exasperated Amber muttering rude things about government departments in general and the Home Office in particular.

In ten minutes the door opened again.

Amber was not prepared for his visitor, and as he sprang awkwardly to his feet, he went alternately red and white. The girl herself was pale, and she did not speak until the door closed behind the warders. That brief space of time gave Amber the opportunity to recover his self-possession.

"I fear that I cannot offer you the courtesies that are due to you," he said. "For the moment my freedom of movement is somewhat restricted."

She thought he referred to his presence in prison, and half smiled at the politeness of a speech so out of all harmony with the grim surroundings.

"You are probably surprised to see me, Mr. Amber," she said. "It was in desperation that I went to the Home Office to endeavour to secure an interview with you—there is no one else in the world knows so much of this expedition and the men who have formed it."

"Did you find any difficulty in obtaining permission?" There was an odd twinkle in Amber's eye which she did not observe.

"None—or almost none," she said. "It was very wonderful."

"Not so wonderful, my lady," said Amber. "I'm an old client: anything to oblige a regular customer."

She was looking at him with pain in her eyes.

"Please—please don't talk like that," she said in a low voice. "You rather hurt me: I want to feel that you are not beyond—help, and when you talk so flippantly and make so light of your—trouble, it does hurt, you know."

He dropped his eyes and, for the matter of that, so did she.

"I am sorry," he said in a quieter tone, "if I have bothered you: any worry on your part has been unnecessary, not," he added with a touch of the old Amber, "that I have not been worth worrying about, but you have not quite understood the circumstances. Now please tell me why you wish to see me; there is a stool—it is not very comfortable, but it is the best I can offer you."

She declined the seat with a smile and began her story.

Her brother had sailed, so also had Lambaire and Whitey, taking with them a copy of the chart.

"I have not worried very much about the expedition," she said, "because I thought that my father's map was sufficiently accurate to lead them to this fabulous river. The Colonial Office officials, whom my brother saw, took this view also."

"Why did he see them?" demanded Amber.

"To get the necessary permission to prospect in British territory—it is a Crown possession, you know. After my brother had arrived in Africa, and I had received a cable to that effect, I had an urgent message from the Colonial Office, asking me to take the chart to Downing Street. I did so, and they made a careful examination of it, measuring distances and comparing them on another map."

"Well?"

"Well," she shrugged her shoulders, "the expedition is futile: if the River of Stars is not in Portuguese territory, it has no existence at all."

"Isn't it in British territory?"

"No, it is well over the border line that marks the boundary between British and Portuguese West Africa."

Amber was puzzled.

"What can I do?" he asked.

"Wait," she went on rapidly, "I have not told you all, for if my father's map is true, the River of Stars is a fable, for they definitely located the spot indicated in his map, and there is neither forest nor river there, only a great dry plateau."

"You told them about the false compass?"

"Lambaire was very frank to me before Francis sailed. He showed me the false and the true and I saw for myself the exact deflection; what is more, I took careful notice of the difference, and it was on this that the Colonial Office worked out its calculations. A cable has been sent to stop my bother, but he has already left the coast with the two men and is beyond the reach of the telegraph."

"Have you got the map with you?"

She took the soiled chart from her bag and offered it to him. He did not take it for his hands were still behind him, and suddenly she understood why and flushed.

"Open it and let me see, please."

He studied it carefully: then he said, "By the way, who told the Colonial Office that I knew all about this business—oh, of course you did."

She nodded.

"I did not know what to do—I have lost my father in that country—for the first time I begin to fear for my brother—I have nobody to whom I can appeal for advice..."

She checked herself quickly, being in a sudden terror lest this thief with his shaven head and his steel-clamped wrists should discover how big a place he held in her thoughts.

"There is something wrong, some mystery that has not been unravelled: my father was a careful man and could not have made a mistake: all along we knew that the river was in British territory."

"The boundary may have been altered," suggested Amber. But she shook her head.

"No, I asked that question: it was demarcated in 1875 and has not been altered."

Amber looked again at the map, then at the girl.

"I will see you to-morrow," he said.

"But—" She looked at him in astonishment. "I may not be able to get permission to-morrow."

A key turned in the lock and the heavy door opened slowly. Outside was the governor with a face as black as thunder, the chief warder and Fells.

"Time's up," said the governor gruffly. Amber looked at the detective and nodded; then called authoritatively to the prison chief.

"Take these handcuffs off, Cardeen," he said.

"What—!"

"Give him the order, Fells," said Amber, and the detective obediently handed a paper to the bewildered man.

"You are suspended from duty," said Amber shortly, "pending an inquiry into your management of this gaol. I am Captain Ambrose Grey, one of His Majesty's inspectors of prisons."

The chief warder's hands were shaking horribly as he turned the key that opened the hinged bar of the handcuffs.

XII. — AMBER SAILS

AMBER went down to Southampton one cheerless day in December, when a grey, sad mist lay on the waters, and all that was land spoke of comfort, of warm snug chimney corners and drawn curtains, and all the sea was hungry dreariness.

He did not expect to see Cynthia when he came to Waterloo, for he had taken a shaky farewell the night before... She had been irritatingly calm and self-composed, so matter-of-fact in her attitude, that the words he had schooled himself to say would not come.—1

He was busily engaged composing a letter to her—a letter to be posted before the ship sailed— and had reached the place where in one sketchy sentence he was recounting his wordly prospects for her information, when she came along the train and found him.

An awkward moment for Amber—he was somewhat incoherent— remarked on the beauty of the day oblivious of the rain that splashed down upon the carriage window—and was conventionally grateful to her for coming to see him off.

He could not have been lucid or intelligent, for he caught her smiling—but what is a man to say when his mind is full of thoughts too tremendous for speech, and his tongue is called upon to utter the pleasantries of convention?"

All too quickly it seemed, the guard's whistle shrilled. "Oh, hang it! " Amber jumped up.

"I am sorry—I wanted to say—Oh, dash it!"

She smiled again.

"You will have plenty of time," she said quietly, "I am going to Southampton."

An overjoyed and thankful man sank back onto his seat as the train drew out of the station. What he might have said is easy to imagine. Here was an opportunity if ever there was one. He spoke about the beauty of the day—she might have thought him rude but for understanding. He spent half an hour explaining how the hatters had sent him a helmet two sizes larger than necessary, and gave her a graphic picture of how he had looked. She was politely interested...

Too quickly the train rattled over the points at Eastleigh and slowed for Southampton town. It was raining, a thin cold drizzle of rain that blurred the windows and distorted the outlines of the buildings through which the train passed slowly on its way to the docks.

Amber heaved a long sigh and then, observing the glimmer of amusement in the girl's eyes, smiled also.

"Rank bad weather, my lady," he said ruefully. "Heaven's weepin', England in mourning at the loss of her son, and all that sort of thing."

"She must bear her troubles," said the girl mockingly, and Amber marvelled that she could be so cheerful under such distressing circumstances— for I fear that Amber was an egotist.

In the great barnlike shed adjoining the quayside they left the carriage and made their way across the steaming quay to the gangway.

"We will find a dry place," said Amber, "and I will deposit you in comfort whilst I speak a few kindly words to the steward." He left her in the big saloon, and went in search of his cabin.

He had other matters to think about—the important matters; matters affecting his life, his future, his happiness. Now if he could only find a gambit— an opening. If she would only give him a chance of saying all that was in his heart. Amber, a young man remarkably self-possessed in most affairs of life, tossed wildly upon a tempestuous sea of emotion, in sight of land, with a very life-line at hand to bring him to a place of safety, yet without courage to grasp the line or put the prow of his boat to shore.

"For," he excused, "there may be rocks that way, and it is better to be uncomfortable at sea than drowned on the beach."

Having all these high matters to fill his mind, he passed his cabin twice, missed his steward and found himself blundering into second class accommodation amongst shivering half-caste folk before he woke up to the fact that his errand was still unperformed.

He came back to the saloon to find it empty, and a wild panic came on him. She had been tired of waiting—there was an early train back to town and she had gone.

He flew out on to the deck, ran up and down companionways innumerable, sprinted along the broad promenade deck to the amazement of stolid quartermasters, took the gangway in two strides and reached the damp quay, then as quickly came back to the ship again to renew his search.

What a hopeless ass he was! What a perfect moon-calf! A picture of tragic despair, he came again to the saloon to find her, very cool and very dry—which he was not.

"Why, you are wet through," was her greeting. Amber smiled sheepishly.

"Yes, lost a trunk, you know, left on the quay— just a little rain— now I want to say something—"

He was breathless but determined as he sat beside her.

"You are to go straight to your cabin and change your clothes," she ordered.

"Don't worry about that, I—"

She shook her head.

"You must," she said firmly, "you will catch all sorts of things, besides you look funny."

A crowning argument this, for men will brave dangers and suppress all manner of heroic desires, but ridicule is a foe from which they flee.

He had an exciting and passionate half-hour, unlocking trunks, and dragging to light such garments as were necessary for the change. For the most part they lay at the bottom of each receptacle and were elusive. He was hot and dishevelled, when with fingers that shook from agitation he fastened the last button and closed the door on the chaos in his cabin.

There was a precious half-hour gone—another was to be sacrificed to lunch—for the ship provided an excellent *déjeuner* for the passengers' friends, and my lady was humanly hungry.

When he came to the covered promenade deck the mails were being run on board, which meant that in half an hour the bell would ring for all who were not travelling to go on shore, and the blessed opportunity which fate had thrown in his way would be lost.

She seemed more inclined to discuss the possibility of his reaching her brother—a pardonable anxiety on her part, but which, unreasonably, he resented. Yet he calmed himself to listen, answering more or less intelligently.

He writhed in silent despair as the minutes passed, and something like a groan escaped from him as the ship's bell clanged the familiar signal.

He rose, a little pale.

"I am afraid this is where we part," he said unsteadily, "and there were one or two things I wanted to say to you."

She sprang up, a little alarmed, he thought— certainly confused, if he judged rightly by the pink and white that came to her cheek.

"I wanted to say—to ask you—I am not much of a fellow as fellows go, and I dare say you think I am a—" He had too many openings to this speech of his and was trying them all.

"Perhaps you had better wait," she said gently.

"I intended writing to you," he went on, "as soon as we touched Sierra Leone—in fact I was going to write from here." A quartermaster came along the deck. "Any more for the shore?" He glanced inquiringly at the pair. "Last gangway's bein' pulled off, m'am."

Amber looked hopelessly down at her. Then he sighed.

"I am afraid I shall have to write after all," he said ruefully, and laughed.

Her smile answered his, but she made no movement.

Again the bell clanged.

"Unless you want to be taken on to the Alebi Coast," he said, half jestingly, "you will have to go ashore."

Again she smiled.

"I want to be taken out to the Alebi Coast," she said, "that is what I have paid my passage money for."

Amber was well-nigh speechless.

"But—you can't—your luggage?"

"My luggage is in my cabin," she said innocently; "didn't you know I was coming with you?"

Amber said nothing, his heart being too full for words.

* * * * *

When they were five days out, and the sugar-loaf mountain of Teneriffe was sinking behind them, Amber awoke to the gravity of the situation.

"I've been a selfish pig," he said, "if I'd had the heart to do it I could have persuaded you to leave the ship at Santa Cruz—you ought not to come."

"*J'y suis—j'y reste!*" she said lazily. She was stretched on a wicker lounge chair, a dainty picture from the tip of her white shoes to the crown of her pretty head.

"I'm an explorer's daughter," she went on half seriously, "you have to remember that, Captain Grey."

"I'd rather you called me Amber," he said.

"Well, Mr. Amber," she corrected, "though it seems a little familiar; what was I saying?"

"You were boasting about your birth," he said. He pulled a chair to her side—" and we were listening respectfully."

She did not speak for some time, her eyes following the dancing wavelets that slipped astern as the ship pushed through the water.

"It is a big business, isn't it?" she said suddenly. "This country killed my father—it has taken my brother—"

"It shall not take you," he said between his teeth, "I'll have no folly of that kind; you must go back. We shall meet the homeward Congo boat at Grand Bassam and I shall transfer you."

She laughed out loud, a long low laugh of infinite amusement.

"By force, I suppose," she rallied him, "or wrapped up in canvas labelled 'Stow away from boilers.' No, I am going to the base of operations— if no further. It is my palaver—that is the right word, isn't it?—much more than yours."

She was wholly serious now.

"I suppose it is," he said slowly, "but it's a man's palaver, and a nasty palaver at that. Before we catch up to Lambaire and his party even—"

He hesitated.

"Even if we do," she suggested quietly; and he nodded.

"There is no use in blinking possibilities," he went on. His little drawl left him and the gentleness in his voice made the girl shiver.

"We have got to face the worst," he said. "Lambaire may or may not believe that the River of Stars is in Portuguese territory. His object in falsifying the compass may have been to hoodwink the British Government into faith in his *bona fides*—you see, we should have believed your father, and accepted his survey without question."

"Do you think that was the idea?" she asked.

Amber shook his head.

"Frankly no. My theory is that the compass was faked so that your father should not be able to find the mine again: I think Lambaire's idea was to prevent the plans from being useful to anybody else but himself—if by chance they fell into other hands."

"But why take Francis?" she asked in perplexity.

"The only way they could get the plan—any way their position was strengthened by the inclusion of the dead explorer's son."

This was the only conversation they had on the subject. At Sierra Leone they transferred their baggage to the Pinto Colo, a little Portuguese coasting steamer, and then followed for them a leisurely crawl along the coast, where, so it seemed, at every few miles the ship came to an anchor to allow of barrels of German rum to be landed.

Then one morning, when a thick white mist lay on the oily water, they came to an anchor off a low-lying coast—invisible from the ship—which was the beginning of the forbidden territory.

"We have arrived," said Amber, an hour later, when the surf-boat was beached. He turned to a tall thin native who stood aloof from the crowd of boatmen who had assisted at the landing.

"Dem Consul, he lib...?"

"Massa," said the black man impressively, "him lib for bush one time—dem white man him lib for bush, but dem bush feller he chop um one time, so Consul him lib for bush to hang um bush feller."

To the girl this was so much gibberish, and she glanced from the native to Amber who stood alert, his eyelids narrow, his face tense.

"How you call um, them white man who go dead?" he asked.

Before the man could answer something attracted his attention and he looked up. There was a bird circling slowly above him.

He stretched out his arms and whistled softly, and the bird dropped down like a stone to the sandy beach, rose with an effort, waddled a step or two and fell over, its great crop heaving.

The native lifted it tenderly—it was a pigeon.

Round one red leg, fastened by a rubber band, was a thin scrap of paper. Amber removed the tissue carefully and smoothed it out.

```
To O. C. Houssas.
```

```
Messrs.  Lambaire  and  White  have  reached  Alebi  Mission
Station.  They  report  having  discovered  diamond  field  and
state Sutton died fever month ago.

(Signed) H. Sanders.
```

He read it again slowly, the girl watching with a troubled face.

"What does it say?" she asked.

Amber folded the paper carefully.

"I do not think it was intended for us," he said evasively.

XIII. — IN THE FOREST

IN the K'hassi backland three men sat at chop. The sun was going down, and a log fire such as the native will build on the hottest day sent up a thin straight whisp of smoke.

The stout man in the soiled ducks was Lambaire, j the thin man with the yellow unshaven face was Whitey. He was recovering from his second attack of fever, and the hand that he raised to his mouth shook suggestively. Young Sutton was a sulky third.

They did not speak as they disposed of the unpalatable river fish which their headman had caught for them. Not until they had finished and had strolled down to the edge of the river, did they break the silence.

"This is the end of it," said Lambaire thickly.

Whitey said nothing.

"Three thousand pounds this expedition has cost, and I don't know how many years of my life," Lambaire continued, "and we're a thousand miles from the coast."

"Four hundred," interrupted Whitey impatiently, "and it might as well be four thousand."

There was a long pause in the conversation.

"Where does this river lead to?" asked Lambaire; "it must go somewhere."

"It goes through a fine cannibal country," said Whitey grimly, "if you're thinking of a short cut to the sea leave out the river."

"And there's no River of Stars—no diamonds: a cursed fine explorer that father of yours, Sutton." He said this savagely, but the boy with his head on his knees, looking wistfully at the river, made no reply.

"A cursed fine explorer," repeated Lambaire. Sutton half turned his head. "Don't quarrel with me," he said drearily; "because if you do—"

"Hey! if I do?" Lambaire was ripe for quarrelling with anybody.

"If you do, I'll shoot you dead," said the boy, and turned his head again in the direction of the river.

Lambaire's face twitched and he half rose—they were sitting on the river bank. "None o' that talk, none o' that talk, Sutton," he growled tremulously; "that's not the sort o'—"

"Oh, shut up!" snarled Whitey, "we don't want your jabber, Lambaire—we want a way out!"

A way out! That is what the search for the river had come to: this was the end of four months' wandering, every day taking them further and further into the bush; every week snapped one link that held them to civilization. They had not reached the Portuguese border, because, long before they had arrived within a hundred miles of the frontier, it was apparent that the map was all wrong. There had been little villages marked upon it which they had not come by: once when a village had been traced, and a tribal headquarters located, they had discovered, as other African travellers had discovered, that a score of villages bearing the same name might be found within a radius of a hundred miles.

And all the time the little party, with its rapidly diminishing band of carriers, was getting further and further into the bush. They had parleyed with the Alebi folk, fought a running fight with the bush people of the middle forest, held their camp against a three day attack of the painted K'hassi, and had reached the dubious security which the broken-spirited slave people of the Inner Lands could offer.

And the end of it was that the expedition must turn back, passing through the outraged territories they ha " forced,

"There is no other way," persisted Lambaire. Whitey shook his head.

A singularly futile ending to a great expedition. I am following the train of thought in Sutton's mind as he gloomed at the river flowing slowly past. Not the way which such expeditions ended in books.

Cynthia would laugh, he shuddered. Perhaps she would cry, and have cause moreover.

And that thief man, Amber; a rum name, Amber —gold, diamonds. No diamonds, no River of Stars: the dream had faded. This was a river. It slugged a way through a cannibal land, it passed over hundreds of miles of cataracts and came to the sea... where there were ships that carried one to England... to London.

He sprang up. "When shall we start?" he asked dully.

"Start?" Lambaire looked up.

"We've got to go back the way we came," said the boy. "We might as well make a start now—the carriers are going—two went last night. We've no white man's food; we've about a hundred rounds of ammunition apiece."

"I suppose we can start to-morrow,M he said listlessly.

* * * * *

Before the sun came up, a little expedition began its weary march coastward.

For three days they moved without opposition; on the fourth day they came upon a hunting regiment of the K'hassi—an ominous portent, for they had hoped to get through the K'hassi country without any serious fighting. The hunting regiment abandoned its search for elephant and took upon itself the more joyous task of hunting men.

Fortunately the little party struck the open plain which lies to the westward of the K'hassi land proper, and in the open they held the enemy at bay. On the fifth day their headman, marching at the rear of the sweating carriers, suddenly burst into wild and discordant song. Sutton and Whitey went back to discover the reason for the outburst, and the man with a chuckle told them that he had seen several devils. That night the headman took a billet of wood, and creeping stealthily upon a carrier with whom he had been on perfectly friendly terms, smashed his skull.

"It is sleeping sickness," said Sutton.

The three white men were gathered near the tree to which the mad headman was bound—not without a few minor casualties among the carriers.

"What can we do?" fretted Lambaire. "We can't leave him—he would starve, or he might get free—that's worse."

Eventually they let the problem stand over till the morning, setting a guard to watch the lunatic.

The carriers were assembled in the morning under a new headman, and the caravan marched, Whitey remaining behind. Lambaire, marching in the centre of the column, heard the sharp explosion of a revolver, and then after a pause another. He shuddered and wiped his moist forehead with the back of his hand.

Soon Whitey caught up with the party—Whitey, pallid of face, with his mouth trembling.

Lambaire looked at him fearfully.

"What did you do?" he whispered.

"Go on, go on," snarled the other. "You are too questioning, Lambaire, you are too prying—you know damn'd well what I have done. Can't leave a nigger to starve to death—hey? Got to do something?" His voice rose to a shrill scream, and Lambaire, shaking his head helplessly, asked no more.

In romances your rascal is so thorough paced a rascal that no good may be said of him, no meritorious achievement can stand to his credit. In real life great villains can be heroic. Lambaire was naturally a coward—he was all the greater hero that he endured the rigours of that march and faced the dangers which every new day brought forth, uncomplainingly.

They had entered the Alebi country on the last long stage of the journey, when the great thought came to Lambaire. He confided to nobody, but allowed the matter to turn over in his mind two whole days.

They came upon a native village, the inhabitants of which were friendly disposed to the strange white men, and here they rested their weary bodies for the space of three days.

On the evening of the second day, as they sat before a blazing fire—for the night air had a nip even in equatorial Africa—Lambaire spoke his mind.

"Does it occur to you fellows what we are marching towards?" he asked.

Neither answered him. Sutton took a listless interest in the conversation, but the eyes of Whitey narrowed watchfully.

"We are marching to the devil," said Lambaire, impressively. "I am marching to the bankruptcy court, and so are you, Whitey. Sutton is marching to something that will make him the laughing-stock of London; and," he added slowly, watching the effect of his words, "that will make his father's name ridiculous."

He saw the boy wince, and went on— " Me and Whitey floated a Company—got money out of the public—diamond mine—brilliant prospects and all that sort of thing—see?"

He caught Whitey nodding his head thoughtfully, and saw the puzzled interest in Sutton's face.

"We are going back—"

"If we get back," murmured Whitey. "Don't talk like a fool," snapped Lambaire. "My God, you make me sick, Whitey; you spoil everything! Get back! Of course we will get back—the worst of the fighting is over. It's marchin' now—we are in reach of civilization—"

"Go on—go on," said Whitey impatiently, "when we get back?"

"When we do," said Lambaire, "we've got to say,'Look here, you people—the fact of it is—'"

"Making a clean breast of the matter," murmured Whitey.

"Making a clean breast of the matter—'there's no mine.'"

Lambaire paused, as much to allow the significance of the situation to sink into his own mind as into the minds of the hearers.

"Well?" asked Whitey.

"Well," repeated the other, "why should we? Look here!"—he leant forward and spoke rapidly and with great earnestness—" what's to prevent our saying that we have located the diamond patch, eh? We can cut out the river—make it a dried river bed —we have seen hundreds of places where there are rivers in the wet season. Suppose we get back safe and sound with our pockets full of garnets and uncut diamonds—I can get 'em in London—"

Whitey's eyes were dancing now; no need to ask him how the ingenious plan appealed to him. But Sutton questioned.

The young's man's face was stiff with resentment. "You are mad, Lambaire," he said roughly. "Do you think that I would go back and lie? Do you imagine that I would be a party to a fraud of that kind—and lend my father's name and memory to it? You are mad."

Neither man had regarded him as a serious factor in the expedition and its object. They did not look for opposition from one whom they had regarded more or less as a creature. Yet such opposition they had to meet, opposition that grew in strength with every argument they addressed to him.

Men who find themselves out of touch with civilization are apt to take perverted moral views, and before they had left the friendly village both Whitey—the saner of the pair—and Lambaire had come to regard themselves as ill-used men.

Sutton's ridiculous scruples stood between them and fortunes; this crank by his obstinacy prevented their reaping the reward of their industry. At the end of a week—a week unrelieved by the appearance of a danger which might have shaken them to a clarity of thought—Sutton was outcast. Worse than that, for him, he developed a malignant form of malaria, and the party came to a halt in a big clearing of the forest. Here, near a dried watercourse, they pitched their little camp, being induced to the choice by the fact that water was procurable a few feet below the surface.

Lambaire and Whitey went for a walk in the forest. Neither of them spoke, they each knew the mind of the other.

"Well?" said Whitey at last.

Lambaire avoided his eye.

"It means ruin for us—and there's safety and a fortune if he'd be sensible."

Again a long silence.

"Is he bad?" asked Lambaire suddenly, and the other shrugged his shoulders.

"No worse than I've been half a dozen times. It's his first attack of fever."

There was another long pause, broken by Whitey.

"We can't carry him—we've got two carriers, and there's another fifty miles to go before we reach a mission station—so the carriers say."

They walked aimlessly up and down, each man intent on his own thoughts. They spoke no more, but returned to their little camp, where a semi-delirious youth moaned and fretted querulously, talking in the main to himself.

Lambaire stood by him, looking down at the restless figure; then he went in search of Whitey.

"This thing has got to be done regularly," he said, and produced a notebook. "I trust you, Whitey, and you trust me—but we will have it down in black and white."

The two memorandums were drawn up in identical terms. Whitey demurred, but signed....

Before the accustomed hour, Whitey woke the coast boy who acted as interpreter and was one of the two remaining carriers.

"Get up," he said gruffly; "get them guns on your head and move quickly."

The native rose sleepily. The fire was nearly out, and he gave it a kick with his bare foot to rouse it to flame.

"None of that," fumed Whitey—he was in an unusual mood. "Get the other man, and trek."

The little party went silently along the dark forest path, the native leading the way with a lantern as protection against possible attacks from wild beasts.

He stopped of a sudden and turned to Lambaire, who shuffled along in his rear.

"Dem young massa, I no lookum."

"Go on," said Whitey gruffly. f< Dem massa he die one time."

The native grunted and continued his way. Death in this land, where men rise up hale in the morning and are buried in sunset, was not a great matter.

They halted at daybreak to eat the meal which was usually partaken of before marching.

The two white men ate in silence—neither looking at the other.

Not until the forest was flooded with the rising sunlight did Whitey make any reference to the events of the night.

"We couldn't leave a nigger behind to starve— and I am cursed if we haven't left a white man," he said, and swore horribly.

"Don't do it—don't say it," implored Lambaire, raising his big hand in protest; "we couldn't—we couldn't do what we did... you know... what we did to the madman.... Be sensible, Whitey... he's dead."

Three days later they reached an outlying mission station, and a heliograph message carried the news of their arrival to a wandering district commissioner, who was " working " a country so flat that heliographic communication was not possible with the coast.

But he had a basket full of carrier pigeons.

* * * * *

Three weeks' rest, soft beds to lie upon, Christian food to eat, and the use of a razor, make all the difference in the world to men of Lambaire's type. He had a convenient memory. He forgot things easily. There came to the mission station a small keen-faced man in khaki, the redoubtable Commissioner Sanders, who asked questions, but in view of the debilitated condition of the mission guests did not press for information. He heard without surprise that the River of Stars had been discovered,—he gathered from the vague description the men gave him of the locality where the discovery had been made that the new diamond field was in British territory—he was disappointed but did not show it.

For no man charged with the well-being of native peoples welcomes the discovery of precious stones or metal in his dominion. Such wealth means wars and the upheaval of new forces. It means the end of a regular condition, and the super-imposition of a hasty civilization.

There have been critics who asked why the Commissioner then and there did not demand a view of the specimens that Lambaire and his confederate brought from the mythical mine. But Sanders, as I have explained elsewhere, was a simple man who had never been troubled with the administration of a mineralized region, and frankly had no knowledge as to what a man ought to do in the circumstances.

"When did Sutton die?" he ask and they told him.

"Where?"

Here they were at fault, for the spot indicated was a hundred miles inland.

Sanders made a rapid calculation.

"It must be nearer than that," he said. "You could not have marched to the mission station in the time."

They admitted the possibility of error and Sanders accepted the admission, having some experience in the unreliability of starved men's memory.

He questioned the carriers, and they were no more explicit.

"Master," said the headman, speaking in the riverian dialect, "it was at a place where there are four trees all growing together, two being of camwood and one of copal."

Since the forests of the Alebi are mainly composed of camwood and gum, the Commissioner was no wiser.

A fortnight after this conversation, Lambaire and Whitey reached the little coast town where Sanders had his headquarters.

XIV. — A HANDFUL O' PEBBLE

TO walk into a room in West Central Africa with your mind engaged on such matters as occupied the minds of Lambaire and Whitey, and to come suddenly upon a man whom you thought was picking oakum in a county gaol, is somewhat disconcerting. Such was the experience of the two explorers. There was a dramatic pause as Amber rose from the Commissioner's lounge chair.

They looked at him, and he looked at them in silence. The mocking smile which they had come to know so well was missing from his face. He was wholly serious.

"Hullo," growled Lambaire. "What is the meaning of this?"

It was not a striking question. For the moment Amber did not speak. The three were alone in the Commissioner's bungalow. He motioned them to seats, and they sat immediately, hypnotized by the unexpectedness of the experience. "What have you done with Sutton?" asked Amber quietly.

They did not answer him, and he repeated the question.

"He's dead," said Whitey. His voice was unnecessarily loud. "He's dead—died of fever on the march. It was very sad; he died... of fever."

For the first time in his life Whitey was horribly frightened. There was a curious note of command in Amber's tone which was difficult to define. It seemed as though this convict had suddenly assumed the function of judge. Neither Whitey nor Lambaire could for the moment realize that the man who demanded information was one whom they had seen handcuffed to a chain of convicts on Paddington station.

"When did he die?"

They told him, speaking in chorus, eagerly.

"Who buried him?"

Again the chorus.

"Yet you had two natives with you—and told them nothing. You did not even ask them to dig a grave." His voice was grim, the eyes that watched them were narrowed until they seemed almost shut.

"We buried him," Lambaire found his voice, because he was white and we were white—see?"

"I see." He walked to the table and took from it a sheet of paper. They saw it was the rough plan of a country, and guessed that it represented the scene of their wanderings.

"Point out the place where he was buried." And Amber laid the map upon the knees of Whitey.

"Show nothing!" Lambaire recovered a little of his self-possession. "What do you insinuate. Amber? Who the devil are you that you should go round askin' this or that?—an old lag too !"

As his courage revived he began to swear—perhaps the courage waited upon the expletives.

"... After goin' through all this!" he spluttered, "an' hunger an' thirst an' fightin'—to be questioned by a crook."

He felt the fierce grip of Whitey's hand on his wrist and stopped himself.

"Say nothin'—more than you can help," muttered Whitey. Lambaire swallowed his wrath and obeyed.

"What is this talk about a diamond field?" Amber went on in the same passionless, level voice. "The Government know of no such field—or such river. You have told the Commissioner that you have found such a place. Where is it?"

"Find out, Amber," shrilled Whitey, "you are clever—find out, like we had to; we didn't get our information by asking people,—we went and looked!"

He groped round on the floor of the half darkened bungalow and found his hat.

"We're leavin' to-morrow," said Whitey, "an' the first thing we shall do when we reach a civilized port is to put them wise to you—eh?

It don't do to have gaolbirds wandering and gallivanting about British Possessions!" He nodded his head threateningly, and was rewarded by that smile which was Amber's chief charm.

"Mr. Whitey!" said Amber softly, "you will not leave to-morrow, the ship will sail without you."

"Eh?"

"The ship will sail minus," repeated Amber. "No Whitey, no Lambaire."

He shook his head.

"What do you mean?"

For answer Amber tapped the foolscap which he had taken back from the protesting hand of Whitey. "Somewhere here," he pointed to a place marked with a cross, "near a dried river bed, a man died. I want evidence of his death and of the manner in which he met it, before I let you go."

There was another pause.

"What do you mean by that, Mr. Amber?" asked Whitey, and his voice was unsteady.

"Exactly what I say," said the other quietly.

"Do you think we murdered him?"

Amber shrugged his shoulders. "We shall know one way or the other before you leave us," he said easily. There was something in his tone which chilled the two men before him.

"I shall know, because I have sent a search party back to the place where you say you left Mr. Sutton," he went on. "Your late interpreter will have no difficulty in finding the spot—he is already on his way."

Lambaire was as white as death.

"We did nothing to Sutton," he said doggedly.

Amber inclined his head.

"That we shall know," he said.

Walking from the bungalow to the hut which the Commissioner had placed at their disposal, Lambaire suddenly stopped and touched his companion's arm.

"Suppose," he gasped, "suppose—"

Whitey shook off the grip. "Don't go mad," he said roughly, "suppose what?"

"Suppose—some wandering native—found him and speared him. We'd get the credit for that."

"My God, I never thought of that! " It gave them both something to think about in the weary days of waiting. They learnt that the word of Amber was law. They saw him once at a distance, but they sought no interview with him. Also they learnt of the presence, at headquarters, of Cynthia Sutton. For some reason this worried them, and they wondered how much she knew.

She knew all, if the truth be told. Dry eyed and pale she had listened whilst Amber, with all the tenderness of a woman, had broken the news the Commissioner had sent.

"I would like to hold out some hope," he said gently, "but that would be cruel; the story has the ring of truth, and yet there is something in it which leads me to the belief that there is something behind it which we do not know." He did not tell her of his suspicions. These he had confided to Sanders, and the little man had sent a party back to make an examination of the place where Sutton was buried.

"White men die very suddenly in the Alebi," said Sanders. "There is every chance that the story is true—yet they are not the kind of men who from any sentimental consideration would take upon themselves the work of burying a poor chap. That's the part I can't believe."

"What will you do when the search party returns?" asked Amber.

"I have thought it out," replied Sanders. "I shall ask them for no report except in the presence of yourself and the men; this enquiry is to be an impartial one, it is already a little irregular."

Weeks passed—weeks of intolerable suspense for Whitey and Lambaire, playing bumble puppy whist in the shade of their hut.

Sanders paid them duty calls. He gave them the courteous attention which a prison governor would give to distinguished prisoners—that was how it struck Lambaire. Then, one morning, an orderly came with a note for them—Their presence was required at " The Residency." No two men summoned from the cells below the dock ever walked to judgment with such apprehension as did these.

They found the Commissioner sitting at a big table, which was the one notable article of furniture in his office.

Three travel-stained natives in the worn blue uniform of police stood by the desk. Sanders was speaking rapidly in a native dialect which was incomprehensible to any other of the white people in the room.

Amber, with Cynthia Sutton, sat on chairs to the right of the Commissioner's desk, and two vacant chairs had been placed on the left of the desk.

It was curiously suggestive of a magistrate's court, where the positions of plaintiff and defendant are well defined.

Lambaire shot a sidelong glance at the girl in her cool white frock and her snowy helmet, and made a little nervous grimace.

They took their seats, Lambaire walking heavily to his.

Sanders finished talking, and with a jerk of his hand motioned his men to the centre of the room.

"I was getting their story in consecutive order," he said. "I will ask them questions and will translate their answers, if it is agreeable to you?"

Whitey coughed to clear his throat, tried to frame an agreement, failed, and expressed his approval with a nod.

"Did you find the place of the four trees?" asked Sanders of the native.

"Lord! we found the place," said the man.

Sentence by sentence as he spoke, Sanders translated the narrative.

"For many days we followed the path the white men came; resting only one day, which was a certain feast day, we being of the Sufi Sect and worshippers of one god," said the policeman. "We found sleeping places by the ashes of fires that the white men had kindled; also cartridges and other things which white men throw away."

"How many days' journey did the white men come?" asked Sanders.

"Ten days," said the native," for there were ten night fires where there was much ash, and ten day fires, and where there was only so much ash as would show the boiling of a pot. Also at these places no beds had been prepared. Two white men travelled together for ten days, before then were three white men."

"How do you know this?" said Sanders, in the vernacular.

"Lord, that were an easy matter to tell, for we found the place where they had slept. Also we found the spot where the third white man had been left behind."

Lambaire's lips were dry; his mouth was like a limekiln as, sentence by sentence, the native's statement was translated.

"Did you find the white master who was left behind?" asked Sanders.

"Lord, we did not find him."

Lambaire made a little choking noise in his throat.

Whitey stared, saying nothing. He half rose, then sat down again.

"Was there a grave?"

The native shook his head.

"We saw an open grave, but there was no man in it." Lambaire shot a swift startled glance at the man by his side.

"There was no sign of the white master?"

"None, lord, he had vanished, and only this left behind." He dived into the inside of his stained blue tunic and withdrew what was apparently a handkerchief. It was grimy, and one corner was tied into several knots.

Cynthia rose and took it in her hands.

"Yes, this was my brother's," she said in a low voice. She handed it to Sanders.

"There is something tied up here," he said, and proceeded to unknot the handkerchief. Three knots in all he untied, and with each untying, save the last, a little grey pebble fell to the table. In the last knot were four little pebbles no larger than the tip of a boy's finger. Sanders gathered them into the palm of his hand and looked at them curiously.

"Do you know what these signify?" he asked Whitey, and he shook his head.

Sanders addressed the native in Arabic.

"Abiboo," he said, "you know the ways and customs of Alebi folk—what do these things mean?"

But Abiboo was at a loss.

"Lord," he said, "if they were of camwood it would mean a marriage, if they were of gum it would mean a journey—but these things signify nothing, according to my knowledge."

Sanders turned the pebbles over with his finger.

"I am afraid this beats me," he began, when Amber stepped forward.

"Let me see them," he said, and they were emptied into his palm.

He walked with them to the window, and examined them carefully. He took a knife from his pocket and scraped away at the dull surface.

He was intensely occupied, so much so that he did not seem to realize that he was arresting the inquiry. They waited patiently—three—five—ten —minutes. Then he came back from the window, jingling the pebbles in his hand.

"These we may keep, I suppose?" he said; "you have no objection?"

Lambaire shook his head.

He was calmer now, though he had no reason to be, as Whitey, licking his dry lips, realized. The next words of the Commissioner supplied a reason.

"You say that you buried Mr. Sutton at a certain spot," he said gravely. "My men find no trace of a grave—save an open grave—how do you explain this?"

It took little to induce panic in Lambaire—Whitey gave him no chance of betraying his agitation.

"I give no explanation," he piped in his thin voice; "we buried him, that's all we know—your men must have mistaken the spot. You can't detain us any longer; it's against the law—what do you accuse us of, hey? We've told you everything there is to tell; and you've got to make up your mind what you are going to do."

He said all this in one breath and stopped for lack of it, and what he said was true—no one knew the fact better than Amber.

"Let me ask you one question," he said. "Did you discover the diamond mine, of which we have heard so little, before or after the—disappearance of Mr. Sutton?"

Lambaire, who was directly addressed, made no reply. It was safer to rely upon Whitey when matters of chronology were concerned.

"Before," said Whitey, after the slightest pause.

"Long before?"

"Yes—a week or so."

Amber tapped the table restlessly—like a man deep in thought.

"Did Mr. Sutton know of the discovery? M

"No," said Whitey—and could have bitten his tongue at the slip; "when the discovery was made he was down with fever," he added.

"And he knew nothing?"

"Nothing."

Amber opened his hand and allowed the four pebbles to slip on to the table.

"And yet he had these," he said.

"What are they to do with it?" asked Whitey.

Amber smiled.

"Nothing," he said, "except that these are diamonds."

XV. — IN THE BED OF THE RIVER

IT was a fortunate circumstance that within three days two homeward bound ships called at the little coast town where the Commissioner for the Alebi district made his headquarters. Fortunate, for it allowed Lambaire and Whitey to travel homewards by one ship, and Cynthia Sutton by the other. Amber went to the beach where the heavy surf-boat waited—to see her off.

"I ought to be 1 king my ticket with you," he said, "or better still follow you secretly, so that when you sit down to dinner to-night—enter Amber in full kit, surprise of lady—curtain."

She stood watching him seriously. The heat the coast had made her face whiter and finer drawn. She was in Amber's eyes the most beautiful woman he had ever seen. Though he could jest, his heart was heavy enough and hungry enough for tears.

"I wish you would come," she said simply, and he knew her heart at that moment.

"I'll stay." He took her hand in both of his, "There's a chance, though it is a faint one, that your brother is alive. Sanders says there is no doubt that those men left him to die—there is no proof that he is dead. I shall stay long enough to convince myself one way or the other."

The boat was ready now, and Sanders was discreetly watching the steamer that lay anchored a mile from the shore in four fathoms of water.

"*Au revoir*," she said, and her lip trembled.

Amber held out his arms to her, and she came to him without fear. He held her tight for the space of a few seconds, and she lifted her face to his.

"*Au revoir*, my love," he whispered, and kissed her lips,

* * * * *

Amber left the next morning for the Alebi, and with him went Abiboo, a taciturn sergeant of Houssas and Sanders' right-hand man.

It was a conventional African journey into the bush.

The monotony of hot marches by day, of breathless humming nights, of village palavers, of sudden tropical storms where low lying yellow clouds came tumbling and swirling across the swaying treetops, and vivid lightnings flickered incessantly through the blue-dark forest.

The party followed the beaten track which led from village to village, and at each little community inquiries were made, but no white man had been seen since Lambaire and Whitey had passed.

On the twenty-eighth day of the march, the expedition reached the place where Lambaire had said Sutton died. Here, in accordance with his plans, Amber established something of a permanent camp.

Accompanied by Abiboo he inspected the spot where the handkerchief and diamonds had been found, and the depression where the " grave " had been located.

"Master," said Abiboo, "it was here that a hole had been dug."

"I see no hole," said Amber. He spoke in Arabic: there was a time when Captain Ambrose Grey had been a secretary of legation, and his knowledge of Arabic was a working one.

An examination of the ground showed the depression to be the dried bed of a watercourse. Amber explored it for a mile in either direction without discovering any sign of the opening which Abiboo had led him to expect. In some places it was overgrown with a thick tangle of elephant grass and a variety of wild bramble which is found in African forests.

"Water has been here," said Abiboo, "but cola cola," which means long ago.

The fact that the grave had disappeared proved nothing. The heavy rains which they had experienced on the march would have been sufficient to wash down the debris and the loose earth which had stood about the hole.

For three weeks Amber pursued his investigations. From the camp he sent messengers to every village within a radius of fifty miles, without finding any trace of Sutton.

Regretfully he decided to give up the search; two of his carriers had gone down with beri-beri, and the rainy season was getting nearer and nearer. Worse than this the Isisi—Alebi folk—were restless. He had had advice of crucifixions and dances, and Sanders had sent him six more soldiers to strengthen his escort.

The occasional storms had been followed by irregular downpours, and he himself had had an attack of fever.

"I will stay two more days," he told Abiboo," if by then I find nothing, we strike camp."

That night, as he sat in his tent writing a letter to Cynthia, there came a summons from Abiboo.

"Master," said the Houssa, "one of my men has heard a shot."

Amber slipped on his jacket and stepped out of the tent.

"Where—in what direction?" he asked. It was pitch dark, and a gentle drizzle of rain was falling.

"Towards the east," said the native.

Amber returned to the tent for his electric lamp and together they stood listening.

Far away they heard a noise like that made by a cat in pain; the long howls came faintly in their direction.

"That is a wounded leopard," said Abiboo. Amber was thinking rapidly. Save for the gentle murmur of rain there was no sound in the forest. It was certainly not the night for a leopard to advertise his presence.

"If there is a white man in the forest," said Amber, "he would come for this." He slipped his revolver from his pocket and fired two shots in the air. He waited, but there came no answer. At intervals of half a minute he emptied the chambers of the weapon without eliciting any reply.

For the greater part of an hour Amber remained listening. The cries of the leopard—if leopard it was —had died down to a whimper and had ceased. There was nothing to be gained by a search that night; but as soon as daylight came, Amber moved out with two Houssa guards and Abiboo.

It was no light task the party had set itself, to beat six square miles of forest, where sapling and tree were laced together with rope upon rope of vegetation. It was well into the afternoon when Abiboo found the spoor of a wild beast.

Following it they came to flecks of dried blood. It might have been—as Amber realized—the blood of an animal wounded by another. Half an hour's trailing brought them to a little clearing, where stretched at the foot of a tree lay the leopard, dead and stiff.

"H'm," said Amber, and walked up to it. There was no sign of the laceration which marks the beast wounded in fight.

"Turn it over."

The men obeyed, and Amber whistled. There was an indisputable bullet wound behind the left shoulder.

Amber knelt down, and with his hunting knife cut down in search of the bullet. He found it after a long search and brought it to light. It was a flattened Webley revolver bullet. He went back to camp in a thoughtful mood that night.

If it was Sutton's revolver, where was Sutton? Why did he hide himself in the forest? He had other problems to settle to his satisfaction, but these two were uppermost in his mind.

The day had been a fine one, and the customary storm had not eventuated. A beautiful moonlight night had followed the most glorious of sunsets. It was such a night as only Africa sees, a night of silver light that touched all things tenderly and beautified them. Amber had seen such nights in other parts of the great Continent, but never had he remembered such as this.

He sat in a camp chair at the entrance of his tent speculating upon the events of the day. Who was this mysterious stranger that went abroad at night? For the matter of that, what had the leopard been doing to invite his death?

He called up Abiboo from the fire round which the Houssas were squatting.

"It is strange to me, Abiboo," he said, "that the white man should shoot the leopard."

"Lord, so I have said to my men," said Abiboo, "and they think, as I, that the leopard was creeping into a place that sheltered the white master."

Amber smoked a reflective pipe. It occurred to him that the place where they had come upon the first blood stains had been near to a similar dried-up water way. When he came to give the matter fuller consideration he realized that it was a continuation of the river bed near which they were encamped. Following its course he might come upon the spot under an hour. It was a perfect night for investigation— at any rate he resolved to make an attempt.

He took with him four soldiers including the sergeant, who led the way with the lamp. The soldiers were necessary, for a spy had come in during the day with news that the warlike folk of the "Little Alebi " had begun to march in his direction.

Though the river bed made a well defined path for the party it was fairly " hard-going." In places where the deputation made an impenetrable barrier they had to climb up the steep banks and make a detour through the forest.

Once they came upon a prowling leopard who spat furiously at the brilliant white glow of the electric lamp and, turning tail, fled. Once they surprised a bulky form that trumpeted loudly and went blundering away through the forest to safety.

After one of these detours they struck a clear smooth stretch.

"It must be somewhere near," began Amber, when Abiboo raised his hand abruptly. "Listen," he whispered.

They stood motionless, their heads bent. Above the quiet of the forest came a new sound.

"Click—click!" It was faint, but unmistakable.

Amber crept forward.

The river bed turned abruptly to the right, and pressing closely to the right bank he dropped to his knees and crawled cautiously nearer the turn. He got his head clear of the bush that obstructed his view and saw what he saw.

In the centre of the river, plain to see in the bright moonlight, a man in shirt and trousers was digging. Every now and again he stooped and gathered the earth in both hands and laughed, a low chuckling laugh that made Amber's blood run cold to hear. Amber watched for five minutes, then stepped out from his place of concealment.

"Bang !"

A bullet whistled past him and struck the bank at his side with a thud.

Quick as thought he dropped to cover, bewildered. The man who dug had had his back to him—somebody else had fired that shot 1

He looked round at the sergeant.

"Abiboo," he said grimly, "this is a bad palaver: we have come to save a man who desires to kill us."

Crawling forward again he peeped out: the man had disappeared.

Taking the risk of another shot Amber stepped out into the open.

"Sutton!" he called clearly. There was no answer.

"Sutton!" he shouted,—only the echo came to him. Followed by his men he moved forward.

There was a hole in the centre of the watercourse, and a discarded spade lay beside it. He picked it up and examined it. The blade was bright from use, the haft was polished smooth from constant handling. He put it down again and took a swift survey of the place.

He was in what was for all the world like a railway cutting. The dead river had worn its deepest channel here. On the moonlit side of the "cutting" he could see no place that afforded shelter. He walked along by the bank which lay in the shadow, moving the white beam of his lamp over its rugged side.

He thought he saw an opening a little way up. A big dead bush half concealed it—and that dead bush was perched at such an angle as to convince Amber that it owed its position to human agency.

Cautiously he began to climb till he lay under the opening. Then swiftly he plucked the dead brush away.

"Bang!"

He felt the powder burn his face and pressed himself closer to the earth. Abiboo in the bed of the river below came with a leap up the side of the bank.

"*Ba—lek!*" shouted Amber warningly.

A hand, grasping a heavy army revolver, was thrust out through the opening, the long black muzzle pointing in the direction of the advancing Houssa. Amber seized the wrist and twisted it up with a jerk.

"Damn!" said a voice, and the pistol dropped to the ground.

Still holding the wrist, Amber called gently, "Sutton!" There was a pause.

"Who are you?" said the voice in astonishment.

"You'll remember me as Amber." There was another little pause.

"The devil you are!" said the voice; "let go my wrist, and I'll come out—thought you were the Alebi folk on the warpath."

Amber released the wrist, and by-and-by there struggled through a grimy tattered young man, indisputably Sutton.

He stood up in the moonlight and shook himself. "I'm afraid I've been rather uncivil," he said steadily, "but I'm glad you've come—to the 'River of Stars.'" He waved his hand towards the dry river bed with a rueful smile.

Amber said nothing.

"I should have left months ago," Sutton went on; "we've got more diamonds in this hole than— Curse the beastly things!" he said abruptly. He stooped down to the mouth of the cave.

"Father," he called softly, "come out—I want to introduce you to a sportsman."

Amber stood dumfounded and silent as the other turned to him.

"My father isn't very well," he said with a catch in his voice; "you'll have to help me get him away."

XVI. — AMBER ON PROSPECTUSES

THE RIVER OF STARS, LTD.

SHARE CAPITAL, £800,000.

100,000 ORDINARY SHARES OF £5 EACH.

30,000 DEFERRED SHARES OF £10 EACH.

DIRECTORS:

AUGUSTUS LAMBAIRE, ESQ. [CHAIRMAN).

FELIX WHITE, ESQ.

THE HON. GRIFFIN PULLERGER.

LORD CORSINGTON.

SUCH was the heading of the prospectus which found its way into every letter-box of every house of every man who had speculated wisely, or unwisely, in stock exchange securities.

Both Lambaire and Whitey shirked the direct appeal to the public which city conventions demand. I think it was that these two men, when they were confronted with a straightforward way and a crooked way of conducting business with which they might be associated, instinctively moved towards the darker method.

When they had arrived in England they had decided upon the campaign; they came with greater prestige than they had ever dared to hope for— the discovery, astonishing as it had been to them at the moment, of the diamonds in Sutton's knotted handkerchief,—gave support to their story, which was all the stronger since the proof of the mine's existence came from the enemy.

On the voyage to England they had grown weary of discussing by what mysterious process, by what uncanny freak of fortune, the stones had been so found, and they had come to a condition of mind where they accepted the fact. The preparation of the prospectus had been a labour of love; there was no difficulty in securing a name or two for the directors. They had had the inestimable advantage of a press sensation. They might, indeed, have chosen the latter-day method of publishing in the newspapers. Their prospectus was very feasible.

There were not wanting critics who were curious as to the exact location of the diamond field of fabulous wealth, but this difficulty they had got over in part by the cunning constitution of the company, which allowed of a large portion of working capital for purposes of exploration; for the further development of "Company Property," and for the opening up of roads to the interior. The Company was registered in Jersey; the significance of that fact will be appreciated by those acquainted with Company procedure.

City editors, examining the prospectus, shook their heads in bewilderment. Some damned it instanter, some saw its romantic side and wrote accordingly. Not a few passed it unnoticed, following the golden precept, "No advertisement: no puff."

There is a type of shareholder who loves, and dearly loves a mystery. He lives in the clouds, thinking in millions. His high spirit despises the 2½ per cent, of safety. He dreams of fortunes to come in the night, of early morning intimations that shares which cost him 3s. 9d. have risen to £99 2s. 6d. He can work out in his head at a moment's notice the profit accruing from the possession of a thousand such shares as these. It was from this class that Lambaire expected much, and he was not disappointed.

The promise of the River of Stars was not explicit; there was a hint of risk—frankly set forth—a cunning suggestion of immense profit.

"Rap-rap!" went the knocker of fifty thousand doors as the weighty prospectus dropped with a thud upon the suburban mat... an interval of a day or so, and there began a trickle of reply which from day to day gathered force until it became a veritable stream. Lambaire, in his multifarious undertakings, had acquired addresses in very much the same way as small boys collect postage stamps. He collected addresses with discrimination. In one of the many books he kept—books which were never opened to any save himself, you might see page after page as closely written as his sprawling caligraphy allowed, the names of " possibles," with some little comment on each victim.

"In many ways, Lambaire," said Whitey, "you're a wonder!"

The big man, to whom approval was as the breath of life, smiled complacently.

They sat at lunch at the most expensive hotel in London, and through the open windows of the luxurious dining-room came the hum of Piccadilly's traffic.

"We've got a good proposition," said Lambaire, and rubbed his hands comfortably, "a real good proposition. We've got all sorts of back doors out if the diamonds don't turn up trumps—if I could only get those stones of Sutton's out of my mind."

"Don't start talking that all over again—you can be thankful that things turned out as they did. I saw that feller Amber yesterday."

With a return to civilization, Amber had receded to the background as a factor. They now held him in the good-natured contempt that the prosperous have for their less prosperous fellows.

There was some excuse for their sudden arrogance. The first batch of prospectuses had produced an enormous return. Money had already begun to flow to the bankers of the "Stars."

"When this has settled down an' the thing's finished," said Whitey, "I'm goin' to settle down too, Lam! The crook line isn't good enough."

They lingered over lunch discussing their plans. It was three o'clock in the afternoon when Lambaire paid the bill, and arm in arm with Whitey walked out into Piccadilly.

They walked slowly along the crowded thoroughfare in the direction of Piccadilly Circus. There was a subject which Lambaire wished to broach.

"By the way, Whitey," he said, as they stood hesitating at the corner of the Haymarket, "do you remember a little memorandum we signed?"

"Memorandum?"

"Yes—in the Alebi forest. I forget how it went, but you had a copy and I had a copy."

"What was it about?"

Lambaire might have thought, had he not known Whitey, that the memorandum had slipped from his mind—but Lambaire was no fool.

He did not pursue the subject, nor advance the suggestion which he had framed, that it would be better for all concerned if the two telltale documents were destroyed. Instead, he changed the subject.

"Amber is in London," he said," he arrived last Saturday."

"What about the girl?"

"She's been back months,"—Lambaire made a little grimace, for he had paid a visit to Pembroke Gardens and had had a chilling reception.

"You wouldn't think she'd lost a brother," he went on, "no black, no mourning, theatres and concerts every night—heartless little devil."

Whitey looked up sharply.

"Who told you that?" he asked.

"One of my fellers," said Lambaire carelessly.

"Oh!" said Whitey.

He took out his watch. "I've got an appointment," he said, and jerked his head to an approaching taxi. "See you at the Whistlers."

Whitey was a man with no illusions. The wonder is that he had not amassed a fortune in a line of business more legitimate and more consistent than that in which he found himself. Since few men know themselves thoroughly well, and no man knows another at all, I do not attempt to explain the complexities of Whitey's mind. He had ordered the taxi-driver to take him to an hotel—the first that came into his head.

Once beyond the range of Lambaire's observation, he leant out of the carriage window and gave fresh instructions.

He was going to see Cynthia Sutton. The difference between Lambaire and Whitey was never so strongly emphasized as when they were confronted with a common danger.

Lambaire shrank from it, made himself deaf to its warnings, blind to its possibilities. He endeavoured to forget it, and generally succeeded.

Whitey, on the contrary, got the closer to the threatening force: examined it more or less dispassionately, prodded it and poked it until he knew its exact strength.

He arrived at the house in Pembroke Gardens, and telling the chauffeur to wait, rang the bell. A maid answered his ring.

"Miss Sutton in?" he asked.

"No, sir." The girl replied so promptly that Whitey was suspicious.

"I've come on very important business, my gel," he said, "matter of life and death."

"She's not at home, sir—I'm sorry," repeated the maid.

"I know," said Whitey with an ingratiating smile, "but you tell her."

"Really, sir, Miss Sutton is not at home. She left London last Friday," protested the girl; "if you write I will forward the letter."

"Last Friday, eh?" Whitey was very thoughtful. "Friday?" He remembered that Amber had returned on Saturday.

"If you could give me her address," he said, "I could write to her—this business being very important."

The girl shook her head emphatically.

"I don't know it, sir," she said. "I send all the letters to the bank, and they forward them."

Whitey accepted this statement as truth, as it was.

Walking slowly back to his taxi-cab, he decided to see Amber. He was anxious to know whether he had read the prospectus.

* * * * *

Many copies of the prospectus had, as a matter of fact, come to Amber's hands.

Peter... a dreamer, dabbled in stock of a questionable character. Amber called to see him one morning soon after his return to England, and found the little man, his glasses perched on the end of his nose, laboriously following the adventures of the explorers as set forth in the prospectus.

Amber patted him on the shoulder as he passed at his back to his favourite seat by the window.

"My Peter," he said, "what is this literature?"

Peter removed his glasses and smiled benignly.

"A little affair," he said—life was a succession of affairs to Peter. "A little affair, Amber. I do a little speculation now and then. I've got shares in some of the most wonderful wangles you ever heard tell of."

Amber shook his head.

"Wangles pay no dividends, my Croesus," he said reproachfully.

"You never know," protested Peter stoutly. "I've got fifty shares in the Treasure Hill of the Aztec Company."

"Run by Stolvetch," mused Amber, "now undergoing five of the longest and saddest in our royal palace at Dartmoor."

"It was a good idea."

Amber smiled kindly.

"What else?" he asked.

"I've got a founder's share in the El Mandeseg Syndicate," said Peter impressively.

Amber smiled again.

"Sunken Spanish treasure ship, isn't it? I thought so, and I'll bet you've got an interest in two or three gold-recovery-from-the-restless-ocean companies?"

Peter nodded, with an embarrassed grin.

"Let me see your prospectus."

The romantic Peter handed the precious document across the table.

Amber read it carefully—not for the first time.

"It's very rum," he said when he had finished, "very, very rum."

"What's rum, Amber?"

The other drew a cigarette case from his pocket: selected one and lit it.

"Everything is rum, my inveterate optimist," he said. "Wasn't it rum to get a letter from me from the wild and woolly interior of the dark and dismal desert?"

"That was rum," admitted Peter gravely. "I got all sorts of ideas from that. There's a tale I've been readin' about a feller that got pinched for a perfe'ly innercent crime." Amber grinned. "He was sent to penal servitude, one day—"

"I know, I know," said Amber, "a fog rolled up from the sea, he escaped from the quarry where he had been workin', friend's expensive yacht waitin' in the offin'—'bang! bang!' warders shootin', bells ringin', an' a little boat all ready for the errin' brother—yes?" Peter was impressed.

"You're a reader, Amber," he said, with a note of respect in his voice. "I can see now that you've read 'Haunted by Fate, or the Convict's Bride.' It's what I might describe as a masterpiece. It's—"

"I know—it's another of the rum things of life— Peter, would you like a job?" Peter looked up over his spectacles. "What sort of a job?"— his voice shook a little. "I ain't so young as I used to be, an' me heart's not as strong as it was. It ain't one of them darin' wangles of yours?"

Amber laughed.

"Nothin' so wicked, my desperado—how would you like to be the companion of a gentleman who is recovering from a very severe sickness: a sickness that has upset his memory and brought him to the verge of madness—" He saw the sudden alarm in Peter's eyes. "No, no, he's quite all right now, though there was a time—"

He changed the subject abruptly.

"I shall trust you not to say a word to any soul about this matter," he said. "I have a hunch that you are the very man for the job—there is no guile in you, my Peter."

A knock at the door interrupted him.

"Come in."

The handle turned, and Whitey entered.

"Oh, here you are," said Whitey.

He stood by the door, his glossy silk hat in his hand, and smiled pleasantly.

"Come in," invited Amber. "You don't mind?" —he looked at Peter. The old man shook his head.

"Well?"

"I've been lookin' for you," said Whitey.

He took the chair Amber indicated.

"I thought you might be here," he went on, "knowing that you visited here."

"In other words," said Amber, "your cab passed mine in the Strand, and you told the driver to follow me at a respectable distance— I saw you."

Whitey was-not embarrassed.

"A feller would have to be wide to get over you, Captain," he said admiringly. "I've come to talk to you about—" He saw the prospectus on the table. "Ah! you've seen it?"

"I've seen it," said Amber grimly—" a beautiful production. How is the money coming in?"

"Not too well, not too well," lied Whitey, with a melancholy shake of the head. "People don't seem to jump at it: the old adventurous spirit is dead. Some of the papers..." he shrugged his shoulders with good-natured contempt.

"Very unbelievin', these organs of public opinion," said the sympathetic Amber, "fellers of little faith, these journalists."

"We didn't give 'em advertisements," explained Whitey—" that's the secret of it."

"You gave the 'Financial Herald' an advertisement," reflected Amber, "in spite of which they said funny things—you gave the 'Bullion and Mining Gazette' a good order, yet they didn't let you down lightly." Whitey changed direction. "What I want to see about," he said slowly, "is this: you've had convincin' proof that we've located the mine—would you like to come into the company on the ground floor?"

The audacity of the offer staggered even Amber. "Whitey," he said admiringly, "you're the last word in refrigeration 1 Come in on the ground floor! Not into the basement, my Whitey I"

"Can I speak to you alone?" Whitey looked meaningly in the direction of Peter, and Amber shook his head.

"You can say what you've got to say here," he said, "Peter is in my confidence."

"Well," said Whitey, "man to man, and between gentlemen, what do you say to this: you Join our board, an' we'll give you £4,000 in cash an' £10,000 in shares?" Amber's fingers drummed the table thoughtfully. "No," he said, after a while, "my interest in the Company is quite big enough." " What company?" asked Whitey. "The River of Stars Diamonds, Ltd.," said Amber.

Whitey leant over the table and eyed him narrowly.

"You've no interest in our Company," he said shortly.

Amber laughed.

"On the contrary," he said, "I have an interest in the River of Stars Diamond Fields, Ltd."

"That's not my Company," said Whitey.

"Nor your Diamond Field either," said Amber.

XVII. — WHITEY HAS A PLAN

WHITEY met Lambaire by appointment at the Whistlers. Lambaire was the sole occupant of the card room when the other entered. He was sitting at one of the green baize-covered tables dressed in evening kit, and was enlivening his solitude with a game of Chinese Patience. He looked up.

"Hullo, Whitey," he said lazily, "aren't you going to dress for dinner?"

Whitey closed the door carefully.

"Nobody can hear us?" he asked shortly.

Lambaire frowned.

"What's wrong?" he asked.

"Everything's wrong." Whitey was unusually vehement. "I've seen Amber."

"That doesn't make everything wrong, does it?"

It was a characteristic of Lambaire's that alarm found expression in petulance.

"Don't bark, Lambaire," said Whitey, "don't get funny—I tell you that Amber knows."

"Knows what?"

"That we didn't find the mine."

Lambaire laughed scornfully.

"Any fool can guess that,—how's he going to prove it?"

"There's only one way," replied Whitey grimly, "and he's found it."

"Well," demanded Lambaire as his friend paused.

"He's located the real mine. Lambaire, I know it. Look here."

He pulled up a chair to the table.

"You know why Amber came out?"

"With the girl, I suppose," said Lambaire.

"Girl nothing— " said Whitey. "He came out because the Government thought the mine was in Portuguese territory—your infernal compasses puzzled 'em, Lambaire, all your cursed precautions were useless. All our schemin' to get hold of the plan was waste of time. It was a faked plan."

"Fake! Fake! Fake!"

Whitey thumped the table with his fist. "I don't attempt to explain it—I don't know whether old Sutton did it for a purpose, but he did it. You gave him compasses so that he couldn't find his way back after he'd located it. Lambaire—he knew those compasses were wrong. It was tit for tat. You gave him a false compass—he gave you a spoof plan."

Lambaire rose.

"You're mad," he said roughly, "and what does it matter, anyway?"

"Matter! Matter!" spluttered Whitey, "you great lumbering dolt! You blind man! Amber can turn us down I He's only got to put his finger on the map and say 'Our mine is here,' to bring our company to ruin. He's takin' the first step tomorrow. The Colonial Office is going to ask us to locate the River of Stars—and we've got to give them an answer in a week."

Lambaire sank back into his chair, his head bent in thought. He was a slow thinker.

"We can take all the money that's come in and bolt," he said, and Whitey's shrill contemptuous laugh answered him.

"You're a Napoleon of finance, you are," he piped; "you're a brain broker! You've got ideas that would be disgustin' in a child of fourteen I Bolt! Why, if you gave any sign of boltin' you'd have half the splits in London round you! You're—"

"Aw, dry up, Whitey," growled the big man, "I'm tired of hearing you."

"You'll be tireder," said Whitey, and his excitement justified the lapse.

"You'll be tireder in Wormwood Scrubbs, servin' the first part of your sentence—no, there's no bolt, no bank, no fencing business; we've got to locate the mine."

"How?"

"Somebody knows where it is—-that girl knows, I'll swear. Amber knows—there's another party that knows—but that girl knows."

He bent his head till his lips were near Lambaire's ear.

"There's another River of Stars Company been floated," he whispered, "and it's the real river this time. Lambaire, if you're a man we've got the whole thing in our hands." Whitey went on slowly, emphasizing each point with the thrust of his finger at Lambaire's snowy shirt front till it was spotted with little grey irregular discs.

"If we can go to the Colonial Office and say, 'This is where we found the mine,' and it happens to be the identical place where Amber's gang say they found it, we establish ourselves and kill Amber's Company."

The idea began to take shape in Lambaire's mind.

"We've announced the fact that we've located the mine," Whitey went on. "Amber's goin' to make the same announcement. We jump in first —d'ye see?"

"I don't quite follow you," said Lambaire.

"You wouldn't," snarled Whitey. "Listen—if we say our mine is located at a certain place, the Colonial Office will ask Amber if there is a diamond mine there, and Amber will be obliged to say, Yes— that's where my mine is! But what chance has Amber got? All along we've claimed that we have found a mine; it's only an eleventh hour idea of Amber's; it is his word against ours—and we claimed the mine first!"

Lambaire saw it now; slowly he began to appreciate the possibilities of the scheme.

"How did you find all this out?" he asked.

"Saw Amber—he dropped a hint; took the bull by the horns and went to the Colonial Office. There's a chap there I know—he gave me the tip. We shall get a letter to-morrow asking us to explain exactly where the mine is. It appears that there is a rotten law which requires the Government to 'proclaim' every mining area."

"I forgot that," admitted Lambaire.

"You didn't know it, so you couldn't have forgotten it," said Whitey rudely. "Get out of these glad clothes of yours and meet me at my hotel in about an hour's time."

"I'll do anything that's reasonable," said Lambaire.

An hour later he presented himself at the little hotel which Whitey used as his London headquarters.

It was situated in a narrow street that runs from the Strand to Northumberland Avenue—a street that contains more hotels than any other thoroughfare in London. Whitey's suite occupied the whole of the third floor, in fine he had three small rooms. From the time Lambaire entered until he emerged from the swing door, two hours elapsed. The conference was highly satisfactory to both men.

"We shall have to be a bit careful," were Lambaire's parting words.

Whitey sniffed, but said nothing.

"I'll walk with you as far as—which way do you go," he asked.

"Along the Embankment to Westminster," said Lambaire.

They walked from Northumberland Avenue and crossed the broad road opposite the National Liberal Club. Big Ben struck eleven as they reached the Embankment. An occasional taxi whirred past. The tramway cars, ablaze with lights and crowded with theatre goers, glided eastward and westward. They shared the pavement with a few shuffling night wanderers. One of these came sidling towards them with a whine.

"...couple o' 'apence... get a night's bed, sir... gnawing hunger...!"

They heard and took no notice. The man followed them, keeping pace with his awkward gait. He was nearest Whitey, and as they reached an electric standard he turned suddenly and gripped the man by the coat. "Let's have a look at you," he said. For one so apparently enfeebled by want the vagrant displayed considerable strength as he wrenched himself free. Whitey caught a momentary glimpse of his face, strong, resolute, unshaven.

"That'll do, guv'nor," growled the man, "keep your hands to yourself."

Whitey dived into his pocket and produced half a crown.

"Here," he said, "get yourself a drink and a bed, my son."

With muttered thanks the beggar took the coin and turned on his heel.

"You're getting soft," said the sarcastic Lambaire as they pursued their way.

"I daresay," said the other carelessly, "I am full of generous impulses—did you see his dial?"

" No."

Whitey laughed.

"Well?"

"A split," said Whitey shortly, "that's all—man named Mardock from Scotland Yard."

Lambaire turned pale.

"What's the game?" he demanded fretfully; "what's he mean, Whitey—it's disgraceful, watching two men of our position!"

"Don't bleat," Whitey snapped; "you don't suppose Amber is leavin' a stone unturned to catch us, do you? It's another argument for doing something quick."

He left his companion at Westminster, and walked back the way he had come. A slow-moving taxi-cab overtook him and he hailed it. There was nobody near to overhear his directions, but he took no risks.

"Drive me to Victoria," he said. Half way down

Victoria Street he thrust his head from the window.

"Take me down to Kennington," he said, and gave an address. He changed his mind again and descended at Kennington Gate. From thence he took a tram that deposited him at the end of East Lane, and from here to his destination was a short walk.

Whitey sought one named Coals. Possibly the man's name had in a dim and rusty past been Cole; as likely it had been derived from the profession he had long ceased to follow, namely that of a coal-heaver.

Coals had served Whitey and Lambaire before and would serve them again, unless one of two catastrophes had overtaken him. For if he were neither dead nor in prison, he would be in a certain public house, the informal club from which his successive wives gathered him at 12.30 a.m. on five days of the week, and at 12 midnight and 11 p.m. on Saturdays and Sundays.

Your small criminal is a creature of habit— a blessed circumstance for the police of our land.

Whitey was fortunate, for he had no difficulty in finding the man.

He was standing in his accustomed corner of the public bar, remarkably sober, and the boy who was sent in to summon him was obeyed without delay.

Whitey was waiting at some distance from the public house, and Coals came to him apprehensively, for Whitey was ominously respectable.

"Thought you was a split, sir," said Coals, when his visitor had made himself known, "though there's nothing against me as far as I know."

He was a tall broad-shouldered man with a big shapeless head and a big shapeless face. He was, for a man of his class and antecedents, extremely talkative.

"How are things going with you, sir?" he rattled on in a dead monotonous tone, without pause or emphasis. "Been pretty bad round this way. No work, it's cruel hard the work's scarce. Never seen so much poverty in me life; blest if I know what will happen to this country unless something's done."

The scarcity of work was a favourite topic with Coals; it was a pet belief of his that he was the victim of an economic condition which laid him on the shelf to rust and accumulate dust. If you asked Coals how it was with him he would reply without hesitation.

"Out of work," and there would be a hint of gloom and resentment in his tone which would convince you that here was a man who, but for the perversity of the times, might be an active soldier in the army of commerce.

"Some say it's the Government," droned Coals, "some say it's Germany, but something ought to be done about it, that's what I say... tramping about from early morn to jewy eve, as the good Book sez..."

Whitey cut him short. They had been walking all this time in the direction of the Old Kent Road. The street was empty, for it was close on half-past twelve, and the reluctant clients of the public-houses were beginning to form in groups about the closing doors.

"Coals," said Whitey, "I've got a job for you."

Coals shot a suspicious glance at him.

"I'm very much obliged to you, Mr. White, sir," he said breathlessly, "an' I'd be glad to take it if my leg was better; but what with the wet weather an' hardships and trouble I've been in..."

"It's a job that will suit you," said Whitey, "not much risk and a hundred pounds."

"Oh," said Coals thoughtfully, "not a laggin' job?"

"That's your business." Whitey was brusque to the point of rudeness. "You've done lagging for less."

"That's true," admitted the man. Whitey searched his pocket and found a sovereign.

"In the course of the next day or two," he said, "I shall send for you—you can read, can't you?"

"Yes, sir, thank God," said Coals, heartily for him, "I've had my schooling and good use I've made of it; I've always been a well-behaved man inside, and never lost a mark."

"Indeed," said Whitey, without enthusiasm. He did not like to hear men talk with such pride of their prison reputations.

They parted at the Kent Road end of the street, and Whitey went to the Embankment by a convenient tramway car. He went to his hotel, but only to get an overcoat, for the night was chilly. In a few minutes he was back on the Embankment, going eastward. He hoped to learn something from the Borough.

Near the end of the thoroughfare wherein Peter resided was a coffee stall. The folks of Red Cow Court were of irregular habits; rising at such hours as would please them and seeking sleep as and when required. Meals in Red Cow Court were so many movable feasts, but there was one habit which gave to the Courtiers a semblance of regularity. Near the end of the court was a coffee stall which took up a position at twelve midnight and removed itself at seven a.m. At this stall the more affluent and the more Bohemian residents might be found in the neighbourhood of one o'clock. Whitey—he possessed a remarkable knowledge of the metropolis, acquired often under stress of circumstance—came to the stall hopefully, and was not disappointed.

With his coat buttoned up to his chin he ordered a modest cup of coffee and took his place in the circle of people that stood at a respectful distance from the brazier of glowing coke. He listened in silence to the gossip of the court, it was fairly innocent gossip, for though there were many in the circle who were acquainted with the inside of his Majesty's prisons, the talk was not of " business."

Crime was an accident among the poorer type of criminal, such people never achieved the dignity of being concerned in carefully-planned coups. Their wrong-doing synchronizes with opportunity, and opportunity that offers a minimum of immediate risk.

So the talk was of how So-and-So ought to take something for that cold of his, and how it would pay this or that person to keep a civil tongue in her head.

"Old Jim's got a job."

"Go on."

"Wonderful, ain't it—he's got a job..."

"See the fire engine to-night?"

"No—where?"

"Up the High Street, two."

"Where they going?"

"New Cut—somewhere."

"What time?"

"About—what time is it, Charley?"

"I dunno. Just when old Mr. Musk was going."

"'S he gone?"

"Went in a four-wheeler—gave Tom a bob for carrying his birds."

"Goo' law! Old Musk gone... in a cab... I bet he's an old miser."

"I bet he is too... very close... he's not gone away for good."

"Where's he gone?"

Whitey, sipping his coffee, edged nearer the speaker.

"Gone to a place in Kent—Maidstone... where the hopping is."

(Oh, indiscreet Peter! bursting with importance!)

"No, it ain't Maidstone—it's a place called Were."

"Well, that's Maidstone—anyway Maidstone's the station."

Whitey finished his coffee and went home to bed.

XVIII. — WHITEY'S WAY

AMBER found the road from Maidstone to Rochester a most pleasant way. There are those who in the early spring might have complained that it erred on the side of monotony, that tiresome winding, climbing and dipping road; although bleak enough with the gaunt Kentish rag rising untidily to a modest eminence on the one hand, and the valley of the Medway showing dimly through a white haze on the other.

Yet Amber found the walk invigorating and desirable, and neither grey skies above, nor the keen gusty wind that drove from the sea seeking one's very marrow, chilled or depressed him.

"We might have driven out," said the girl who was with him—her presence explained his oblivion to all else. "I'm so afraid that the weather—"

"Produces complications in the poor African >traveller," said he, and laughed. "Peter gave me a long lecture on the same subject. It appears that a hero of his was subject to brain fever as a result of a sudden change of climate—though that can't be true, for heroes are not affected by the weather."

"I like your Peter," she said, after a pause.

"He's a rum bird," confessed Amber.

"Father likes him too," she went on, and sighed. "Do you think father will ever be well again?"

Amber was a long time framing a reply, so long that she stopped.

"I wish you would tell me," she said quietly.

"I want to tell you," he said. "I was trying to put my most private thoughts into words. Yes," he considered again. "Yes, I believe he will get better."

"He is not—" She did not finish the sentence.

"No, he is not—mad, as madness is understood. He has an obsession—he is so full of one happening that everything has stood still since then."

"He has lost his memory—and yet he remembers me and the River of Stars."

They walked on in silence, both too much engaged in their own thoughts for conversation.

The problem of Sutton the explorer was one which had occupied no small amount of their waking thoughts. The house Cynthia had taken stood back from the road. It had originally been a farmhouse, but a succession of leisured tenants had converted it into a comfortable little mansion, and with its four acres of wooded grounds it made an admirable retreat.

Frank Sutton was sitting before a crackling wood fire, a book on his knees. He looked up with a smile as they entered.

His experience had made a man of him—the fact had never struck Amber so forcibly as it did at that moment. His face was tanned and thin, he had lost the boyish roundness of cheek, and lost too the air of impatience which had distinguished him when Amber had first met him.

"What news?" he asked.

Amber stretched his hands to the blazing fire.

"To-morrow the Colonial Office will ask Lambaire to locate his mine," he said. "I fear my Lambaire will experience a difficulty."

"I think he will," said the other drily. "How long will he be given?"

"A week, and if no explanation is made at the end of that time the Colonial Office will issue a statement casting doubt upon Lambaire's *bona fides*."

"An unusual course," said Sutton.

"An unusual situation, my intrepid explorer," rejoined Amber.

Sutton grinned.

"Don't rot me," he pleaded. "I feel I'm rather a pup."

Amber looked at him with a kindly eye.

"We all pass through the furniture-gnawing stage," he said. "Really, I think you're a rather wonderful kid."

The boy coloured, for there was a note of sincerity in the other's voice.

"Where is your father?" Amber asked suddenly.

"In the grounds with your friend; really, it was an inspiration to send our friend—what is his name—Musk?"

"Peter—you must call him Peter," said Amber. He rose and walked to the French window that opened on to the lawn.

"Peter interests the governor no end," Sutton went on. "He's a perfect library of romance."

"Let us go out and meet them," said Amber.

They walked towards the little walled garden where the explorer found his recreation, and came upon the two unexpectedly.

Peter with a stick was illustrating a story he was telling, and the bent man with the straggling beard and the seamed face stood by, nodding his head gravely at the other.

"Sir Claude," Peter was saying, "was holding the bridge here, so to speak, and Sir Reginald was crossin' the moat there; the men-at-arms was a hurlin' down stones from the battlements, and Lady Gwendoline, sword in hand, defended the White Tower. At that minute, when the heroic youth was a urgin' his valiant archers forward, there arose a loud cry 'St. George and England!'—you understand me, Mr. Sutton? There was no idea that the King's army was so close."

"Perfectly," said the explorer, "perfectly, Mr. —er—perfectly. I remember a similar experience when we were attacking the Mashangonibis in '88 —I—I think I remember."

He passed his hand over his eyes wearily.

"Father," said Frank gently, "here is our friend Captain Grey."

The explorer turned sharply.

"Captain Grey?" he half queried, and held out his hand.

Some fugitive memory of Amber flickered across his mind.

"Captain Grey; I'm afraid my son shot at you !"

"It is of no account, sir," said Amber.

The only association the sick man had with Amber was that other dramatic meeting, and though they met almost daily, the elder Sutton had no comment to offer than that.

Day by day, whether he greeted him in the morning at breakfast, or took leave of him at night, the explorer's distressed, "I am afraid my son shot at you," was the beginning and the end of all conversation.

They walked slowly back to the house, Amber and Peter bringing up the rear.

"He's more sensible, Mr. Amber," said Peter. "He seems to have improved durin' the last two days."

"How long has he had the benefit of your society, my Peter?" asked the other.

"Two days," replied the unconscious Mr. Musk.

Amber had an opportunity of studying the old man as they sat at tea—the meals at White House were of a democratic character.

Old he was not as years went, but the forest had whitened his hair and made deep seams in his face. Amber judged him to be of the same age as Lambaire.

He spoke only when he was addressed. For the greater part of the time he sat with his head sunk on his breast deep in thought, his fingers idly tapping his knee.

On one subject his mind was clear, and that was the subject which none cared to discuss with him— the River of Stars.

In the midst of a general conversation he would begin talking quickly, with none of the hesitation which marked his ordinary speech, and it would be about diamonds.

Amber was giving an account of his visit to London when the old man interrupted him. At first his voice was little above a whisper, but it grew in strength as he proceeded.

"... there were a number of garnets on the ground," he said softly, as though speaking to himself. "There were also other indications of the existence of a diamond pipe... the character of the earth is similar to that found in Kimberley and near the Vaal River... blue ground, indubitable blue ground... naturally it was surprising to find these indications at a place so far remote from the spot wherein our inquiries had led us to believe the mine would be located."

They were silent when he paused. By and bye he went on again.

"The rumours of a mine and such specimens as I had seen led me to suppose that the pipe itself led to the north-westward of the great forest, that it should be at the very threshold of the county rather than at the furthermost border illustrates the uncertainty of exploration... uncertainty... uncertainty? that is hardly the word, I think..."

He covered his eyes with his hand.

Though they waited he said no more. It was a usual ending to these narratives of his; some one word had failed him and he would hesitate, seeking feebly the exact sentence to convey a shade of meaning, and then relapse into silence.

The conversation became general again, and soon after Mr. Sutton went to his room.

"He's better," said Amber heartily, as the door closed upon the bent figure. "We get nearer and nearer to the truth about that discovery of his."

Frank nodded.

"You might have thought that all those months when he and I were alone in the forest, I should have learnt the truth," he said. "Yet from the moment he found me lying where that precious pair of scoundrels left me to the night you discovered us both, he told me nothing."

Amber waited until Peter had bustled away importantly—he took very kindly to the office of nurse—and the three were left together.

"When did you first realize the fact that he had discovered the River of Stars?"

Frank Sutton filled his pipe slowly.

"I don't know when I realized it," he said. "The first recollection I have is of somebody bending over me and giving me a drink. I think that he must have given me food too. I was awfully weak at the time. When I got better I used to lie and watch him scratching about in the bed of the river."

"He was quite rational?"

"Quite, though it used to worry me a bit, when he would bring me a couple of pebbles and beg of me to take great care of them. To humour him I kept them; I used to make a great show of tying them up in my pocket handkerchief, never realizing for a moment that they were diamonds."

"And all this time, Frank, you knew it was father?"

It was the girl who spoke, and Frank nodded again.

"I don't know how I knew, but I knew," he said simply. "I was only a child when he went out, and he has changed from the man I remembered. I tried to persuade him to trek to the coast, but he would not move, and there was nothing to do but to stay and chance getting hold of a native to send to the coast with a message. But the natives regarded the place as haunted, and none came near, not even the hunting regiments. And the curious thing was," he said thoughtfully, "that I did not believe the stones were anything but pebbles."

He got up from the deep chair in which he was sitting.

"I'm going to leave you people for a while— you'll find me in the library."

"I'll go with you for a moment, if you will excuse me," said Amber, and the girl smiled her assent.

When the library door had closed behind them: "Sutton," said Amber, "I want you to be jolly careful about that prospectus—you got my wire?"

"Yes, you wired me not to send the copy to the printers. Why?"

"It contains too much information that would be valuable to Lambaire," said the other. "It contains the very information, in fact, that he would give his head to obtain."

"I never thought of that," said Sutton; "but how could he get it from a little country printer's?"

"I don't think he could get it, but Whitey would. To-morrow or to-day the Colonial Office asks Lambaire to locate his mine—we want to make sure that he does not secure his information from us."

"I take you," said the young man with a cheery nod. "I'm making a copy of the map you prepared, and to-morrow we'll send it to the Colonial Office."

Amber returned to the girl. She was sitting in the corner of the settee which was drawn up at right angles to the fire-place.

She screened her face from the blaze with an opened fan, and he saw little save what an emulating flame leaping higher than its fellows, revealed.

"I want to talk to you seriously," he said, and took his seat at the other end of the couch.

"Please don't talk too seriously; I want to be amused," she said.

There was silence for a few minutes, then:

"I suppose you realize," he said, "that within a week or so you will be the daughter of a very rich man?"

He could not see her face distinctly in the half light, but he thought he saw her smile.

"I have not realized it," she replied quietly, "but I suppose that you are right. Why?"

"Why? Oh, nothing—except that I am not immensely wealthy myself."

She waited for him to go on.

"You see?" he suggested after a while.

She laughed outright.

"I see all there is to be seen, namely, that father will be very rich, and you will not be as rich. What else do you wash me to see?"

He wished her to see more than he cared for the moment to describe, but she was blandly obstinate and most unhelpful.

"I hate being conventional," he said, "more than I hate being heroic. I feel that any of Peter's heroes might have taken the line I take—and it is humiliating. But I—I want to marry you, dear, and you have of a sudden become horribly rich."

She laughed again, a clear whole-hearted laugh of girlish enjoyment.

"Come and sit by me," she commanded; "closer..."

* * * * *

"Do you ever go to bed, my dear?" asked Frank Sutton from the doorway. "It is past eleven o'clock, and Peter and I are bored with one another."

He walked across the room and jabbed the fire.

"And you've let the fire go out, you wretched people."

Cynthia rose guiltily.

"I'm afraid," she faltered, "Captain Grey—

"I'm afraid you have," agreed her brother, as with a smile he kissed her. "Say good-night to Amber: father is asleep."

They heard the rustle of her skirts as she went through the hall to the stairs.

"Talking with Peter?" questioned Amber. "I thought you were working most industriously in your library."

Sutton was poking the fire vigorously.

"Finished that an hour ago; how long do you think you people have been gassing?"

Amber discreetly hazarded no opinion.

"I found Peter tremendously interesting," Sutton said with a laugh. "The little room we have given him looks like nothing so much as a newsagent's —one of those newsagents that specialize in the pernicious literature beloved of youth."

"'Ware hasty judgment," said Amber gravely. "these pernicious—"

There was a hasty step in the hall, the door opened and Cynthia came in a little white of face.

Amber took a quick step forward.

"What is it?" he asked.

"Father is not in his room," she said breathlessly.

"I went in to say good night—he has not been to bed—"

The three looked at each other.

"He is in the garden, I expect," said Frank uneasily. "He has gone out before, though I've begged him not to."

He went out into the hall and took an electric hand lamp that stood on the hall-stand. Amber drew the curtains and opening the French window stepped out.

The girl threw a shawl round her shoulders and followed.

"There's another lamp in the study. Amber," said Sutton; and Amber with a nod strode through the room and down the passage that led to the library.

He found the lamp, turned out the light, and rejoined the others.

A thin fog overhung the country-side and shrouded the grounds, but it was not so thick that it offered any obstacle to their search.

The circuit of the grounds took them very little time. There was no sign of the explorer.

At the furthermost corner of the little estate was a wicket gate which opened to a narrow lane leading from the main road to the Nigerhill Road, and toward this the search party made. As they drew near Amber smothered an oath. The wicket was wide open.

In the circle of light the lamps threw upon the weather-stained door a fluttering white paper attracted their attention.

It was a half-sheet of note-paper fastened by a drawing-pin, and Amber raised his lamp and read—

"*They have took him to the quarry on the Rag. Follow quickly. Turn to the right as you get out of the gate and follow the road up the hill. Go quickly and you can save everything.*

A Friend."

"Wait a moment."

Amber held the other's arm as he made for the lane.

"Don't delay for God's sake, Amber I " cried Sutton fretfully; "we may be in time."

"Wait," commanded Amber sharply.

He flashed his lamp on the ground. The soil was of clay and soft. There were footmarks—of how many people he could not tell. He stepped out into the road. The ground was soft here with patches of grass. Whoever had passed through the wicket had by good fortune or intention missed the soft patches of clay, for there was no recent footprint.

"Come along!" Sutton was hurrying up the road and Amber and the girl followed.

"Have you got a gun?" asked Amber.

For answer Sutton slipped a Smith-Wesson [from his pocket.

"Did you expect this?" asked the girl by his side.

"Something like it," was the quiet answer. 41 Until we had settled this business I insisted that we should all be armed—I know Whitey."

Sutton fell back until he was abreast of them.

"I can see no sign of footmarks," he said, "and I'm worried about that message."

"There is one set of footprints," said Amber shortly.

His light had been searching the road all the time. "As to the message I am more puzzled than worried. Hullo, what is that?"

In the middle of the road lay a black object and Sutton ran forward and picked it up.

"It is a hat," he said. "By Heaven, Amber, it is my father's !"

"Oh," said Amber shortly and stopped dead.

They stood for the space of a few seconds.

"I'm going back," said Amber suddenly.

They stared at him.

"But—" said the bewildered girl, "but—you are not going to give up the search?"

"Trust me, please," he said gently. "Sutton go ahead; there are some labourer's cottages a little way along. Knock them up and get assistance. There is a chance that you are on the right track— there is a bigger chance that I am. Any way it will be less dangerous for Cynthia to follow you than to return with me."

With no other word he turned and went running back the way he came with the long loping stride of a cross-country runner.

They stood watching him till he vanished in the gloom.

"I don't understand it," muttered Frank. The girl said nothing; she was bewildered, dumfounded. Mechanically she fell in by her brother's side. He was still clutching the hat.

They had a quarter of a mile to go before they reached the cottages, but they had not traversed half that distance before in turning a sharp bend of the lane they were confronted by a dark figure that stood in the centre of the road.

Frank had his revolver out in an instant and flashed his lamp ahead.

The girl, who had started back with a heart that beat more quickly, gave a sigh of relief, for the man in the road was a policeman, and there was something very comforting in his stolid, unromantic figure.

"No, sir," said the constable, "nobody has passed here."

"A quarter of an hour ago?" suggested Frank.

"Not during the last three hours," said the policeman. "I thought I heard footsteps down the lane the best part of an hour since, but nobody has passed."

He had been detailed for special duty, to detect poachers, and he had not, he said, moved from the spot since seven o'clock—it was then eleven.

Briefly Frank explained the situation.

"Well," said the man slowly, "they couldn't have brought him this way—and it is the only road to the quarry. Sounds to me like a blind. If you'll wait whilst I get my bicycle, which is behind the hedge, I'll walk back with you."

On the way back Frank gave him such particulars as he thought necessary.

"It's a blind," said the man positively. "Why should they take the trouble to tell you which way they went? You don't suppose, sir, that you had a friend in the gang?"

Frank was silent. He understood now Amber's sudden resolve to return.

The road was down-hill and in ten minutes they were in sight of the house.

"I expect Peter—" began Frank.

Crack!—Crack!

Two pistol shots rang out in the silent night.

Crack—crack—crack!

There was a rapid exchange of shots and the policeman swung himself on to the cycle.

"Take this!"

Frank thrust his revolver into the constable's hand.

At the full speed the policeman went spinning down the hill and the two followed at a run.

No other shots broke the stillness and they arrived out of breath at the wicket gate to find Amber and the constable engaged in a hurried consultation.

"It's all right."

Amber's voice was cheery.

"What of father?" gasped the girl.

"He's in the house," said Amber. "I found him gagged and bound in the gardener's hut at the other end of the garden."

He took the girl's trembling arm and led her toward the house.

"He went out for a little walk in the grounds," he explained, "and they pounced on him. No, they didn't hurt him. There were three of the rascals."

"Where are they?" asked Frank.

"Gone—there was a motor-car waiting for them at the end of the lane. The policeman has gone after them in the hope that they have a breakdown."

He led the way to the sitting-room.

"Peter is with your father. Sit down, you want a little wine, I think"—her face was very white— " I'll tell you all about it. I didn't quite swallow that friendly notice on the wicket. I grew more suspicious when I failed to see any footmarks on the road to support the abduction theory. Then of a sudden it occurred to me that the whole thing was a scheme to get us out of the house whilst they had time to remove your father.

"When I got back to the wicket I made another hurried search of the garden and happed upon the tool-house by luck. The first thing I saw was your father lying on a heap of wood trussed and gagged. I had hardly released him when I heard a voice outside. Three men were crossing the lawn toward the wicket. It was too dark to see who they were, but I ran out and called upon them to stop."

"We heard firing," said the girl.

Amber smiled grimly.

"That was their answer," he said; "I followed them to the road. They fired at me again, and I replied. I rather fancy I hit one."

"You are not hurt?" she asked anxiously.

"My lady," said Amber gaily, "I am unscathed."

"But I don't understand it," persisted Frank. "What did the beggars want to take the governor for?"

Amber shook his head.

"That is beyond my—" He stopped suddenly.

"Let us take a look at the library," he said, and led them to the room.

"Hullo, I thought I turned this light out!"

The light was blazing away, the gas flaring in the draught made by the open door.

Well might it flare, for the window was open. So, too, was the door of the safe hanging wretchedly on one hinge.

Amber said nothing—only he whistled.

"So that was why they lured us from the house," he said softly. "This is Whitey's work, and jolly clever work too."

XIX. — AMBER RUNS AWAY

"I WISH you would let me come with you," she begged the young man, but Amber shook his head.

"You stay here," he said. He was dressed in a thick motor coat and a tweed cap was pulled down over his forehead. The girl had made him some tea and prepared a little meal for him.

He looked at his watch. "One o'clock," he said, "and here's the car." The soft hum of a motor-car as it swung in a circle before the door of the house came to them. "I'm afraid I'm late, sir."

It was the constable, who lifted his cycle from the tonneau as he spoke, "but I had some difficulty in collecting the people together, and my report at the station took me longer than I thought. We have wired to headquarters, and the main roads leading into London are being watched."

"It will probably be too late," replied Amber, "though they could hardly do the journey under an hour and a half."

He took a brief farewell of the girl and jumped into the car by the side of the driver. In a few minutes he was being whirled along the Maidstone Road.

"It is a nearer way," explained the driver, "we get on the main road. To reach London through Rochester means a bad road all the way, and a long journey."

The car was a fast one and the journey lacked interest. It was not until they reached the outskirts of London that their progress was checked.

Turning into the Lewisham High Road, a red lamp was waved before them and they pulled up to discover two policemen. Amber had no difficulty in establishing his identity. Had anything been seen of the other car?

"No, sir," said the sergeant; "though a car with four men passed through the Blackwall Tunnel at half-past twelve—before the special police had arrived to watch it. Our people believed from the description you sent that this was the party you are looking for."

Amber had taken a chance when he had circulated a faithful description of Whitey.

He thanked the sergeant and the car moved towards London. He had taken the precaution of locating Lambaire and Whitey, and at half-past three the car stopped at the end of the street in which the latter's hotel was situated.

"You will find a coffee stall at the end of Northumberland Avenue," he said. "Get yourself some food and be back here in a quarter of an hour."

The street was empty and the hotel as silent as the grave. There had been no rain in London that night nor on the previous day, and the pavement was quite dry. Amber stood for a while before he rang the night bell, and with his little lamp examined the hearthstoned steps that led to the door.

There was no mark to indicate the recent arrival of one who had been walking in clay.

He pushed the button and to his surprise the door was almost immediately opened. The night porter, usually the most lethargic of individuals, was alert and wakeful. Evidently it was not Amber he was expecting, for he suddenly barred the opening.

"Yes, sir?" he queried sharply. "I want a room for the night," said Amber. "I've just arrived from the Continent."

"You're late, sir," said the man suspiciously, "the Continental was in on time at eleven."

"Oh, I came by way of Newhaven," responded Amber carelessly. He trusted to the porter's ignorance of this unfamiliar route.

"I don't know whether we've got a room," said the man slowly. "Any baggage?" " I've left it at the station." Amber put his hand into his breast pocket and took out a flat wad of bank-notes. He detached one and handed it to the man.

"Don't keep me talking all night, my good chap," he said good-humouredly. "Take this fiver on account and deduct a sovereign for the trouble I have given you." The man's attitude of hostility changed. "You quite understand, sir," he said as he led the way up the somewhat narrow stairs, "that I have to be—"

"Oh quite," interrupted Amber. "Where are you going to put me—second floor?"

"The second floor is engaged, sir," said the porter. "In fact I was expecting the gentleman and his friend at the moment you rang."

"Late bird, eh?" said Amber.

"He's been in once to-night—about an hour ago—he had to go out again on business."

On the third floor Amber was shown the large front room to his entire satisfaction—for the fact that such a room was available told him that he had the entire floor to himself.

The porter lit the fire which was laid in the grate.

"Is there anything else you want, sir?"

"Nothing, thank you."

Amber followed the man to the landing and stood there as he descended.

The porter stopped half-way down, arrested by the visitor's irresolute attitude.

"You are sure there is nothing I can do for you. sir—cup of tea or anything?"

"Nothing, thank you," said Amber, slowly removing his coat.

A little puzzled, the man descended.

Amber wanted something very badly, but he did not tell the man. He wanted to know whether the stairs creaked, and was gratified to find that they did not.

He waited a while till he heard the slippered feet shuffling on the paved hall below.

There was no time to be lost. He kicked off his shoes and noiselessly descended to the second floor.

There were three rooms which he judged communicated. One of these was locked. He entered the other two in turn. The first was a conventional sitting-room and opened through folding doors to a small bedroom.

From the appearance of the shaving apparatus on the dressing-table and the articles of dress hanging in the wardrobe, he gathered that this was Whitey's bedroom. There was a door leading to the front-room, but this was locked.

He crept out to the landing and listened.

There was no sound save a far-away whistling which told of the porter's presence in some remote part of the building—probably in the basement.

To open the front door which led to the landing might mean detection; he resolved to try the door between the two rooms.

There was a key in the lock, the end of it projected an eighth of an inch beyond the lock on the bedroom side.

Amber took from his coat pocket a flat wallet and opened it. It was filled with little tools. He selected a powerful pair of pliers and gripped the end of the key. They were curious shaped pliers, for their grip ran at right angles to their handles. The effect was to afford an extraordinary leverage.

He turned the key cautiously.

Snap!

The door was unlocked.

Again he made a journey to the landing and listened. There was no sound.

He gathered his tools together, opened the door, and stepped into the room. It had originally been a bedroom. He gathered as much from the two old-fashioned bed-pulls which hung on one wall. There was a big table in the centre of the room, and a newspaper or two. He looked at the dates and smiled—they were two days old. Whitey had not occupied that room the two days previous. Amber knew him to be an inveterate newspaper reader. There were half a dozen letters and he examined the post-marks—these too supported his view, for three had been delivered by the last post two nights before.

A hasty examination of the room failed to discover any evidence that the stolen papers had been deposited there. He slipped his hand between bed and mattress, looked through contents of a despatch box, which strangely enough had been left unlocked.

Though the room was comfortably furnished there were few places where the papers could be concealed.

Whitey must have them with him. Amber had hardly hoped to discover them with such little trouble. He had turned back the corner of the hearthrug before the fireplace, and was on the point of examining a pile of old newspapers which stood on a chair in the corner of the room, when he heard footsteps in the street without.

They were coming down the street—now they had stopped before the hotel. He heard the far-off tinkle of a bell and was out of the room in a second. He did not attempt to lock the door behind him, contenting himself with fastening it.

There were low voices in the hall below, and interchange of speech between the porter and the new arrivals, and Amber nimbly mounted to the floor above as he heard footsteps ascending.

It was Whitey and Lambaire. He heard the sibilant whisper of the one and the growl of the other.

Whitey unlocked the landing door and passed in, followed by Lambaire. Amber heard the snick of the lock as Whitey fastened it behind him.

He heard all this from the upper landing, then when silence reigned again he descended.

Noiselessly he opened the bedroom door, closing it again behind him.

The communicating door was of the conventional matchwood variety, and there was no difficulty, though the two men spoke in low tones, in hearing what they said.

Whitey was talking.

"...it surprised me... old man... thought he was dead..." and he heard the rumble of Lambaire's expression of astonishment. "...providential... seeing him in the garden... scared to death..."

Amber crouched closer to the door. It took him some time before he trained his ear to catch every word, and luckily during that time they talked of things which were of no urgent importance.

"And now," said Whitey's voice, "we've got to get busy."

"Coals is in no danger?" asked Lambaire.

"No—little wound in the leg... that swine Amber..."

Amber grinned in the darkness.

"Here is the prospectus they were drawing up."

The listener heard the crackling of paper and then a long silence. The men were evidently reading together.

"M—m!" It was Lambaire's grunt of satisfaction he heard. "I think this is all we want to know —we must get this copied at once. There won't be much difficulty in placing the mine... oh, this is the map..."

There was another long pause.

Amber had to act, and act quickly. They were gaining information which would enable them to describe the position of the mine, even if they succeeded in making no copy of the little map which accompanied the prospectus.

He judged from the indistinct tone of their voices that they were sitting with their backs to the door behind which he crouched.

Lambaire and Whitey were in fact in that position.

They sat close together under the one electric light the room possessed, greedily absorbing the particulars.

"We shall have to check this with a bigger map," said Whitey. "I don't recognize some of these places—they are called by native names."

"I've got a real good map at my diggings," Lambaire said. "Suppose you bring along these things. It isn't so much that we've got to give an accurate copy of this plan—we've got to be sure in our own minds exactly where the 'pipe' is situated."

"That's so," said the other reluctantly. "It ought to be done at once. Amber will suspect us and we shall move in a Haze of Splits by this time to-morrow."

He folded up the documents and slipped them into a long envelope. Then he stood thinking.

"Lammie," he said, "did you hear the porter say that a visitor had come during the night?"

"Yes, but that's usual, isn't it?"

Whitey shook his head.

"Unusual," he said shortly," dam' unusual."

"Do you think—?"

"I don't know. I'm a bit nervy," said the other, "but the visitor has been on my mind ever since I came in. I'm going up to have a look at his boots."

"Why?"

"Don't be a fool, and don't ask foolish questions," snarled Whitey. "Visitors put their boots outside the door, don't they? You can tell a lot from a pair of boots."

He handed the envelope containing the stolen prospectus to his companion.

"Take this," he said," and wait till I come down."

He unlocked the door and mounted the stairs cautiously.

Lambaire waited there.

"Lambaire!" hissed a voice from the open door.

"Yes."

"Give me the envelope, quick."

A hand, an eager demanding hand, reached through the little gap.

"Stay where you are—give me the envelope."

Quickly Lambaire obeyed. The hand grasped the envelope, another closed the door quickly, and there was silence.

"Now what the devil is wrong," muttered the startled Lambaire. He felt himself turning pale. There had been a hint of imminent danger in the urgency of the voice. He waited, tense, alert, fearful; then he heard quick steps on the stairs, and Whitey dashed into the room.

"Nobody there," he said breathlessly. "A pair of shoes covered with mud and a pair of gloves— it's Amber."

"Amber !"

"He's followed us—let's get out of this quick. Give me the envelope."

Lambaire went white.

"I—I gave it to you," he stammered.

"You liar!" Whitey was in a white heat of fury. "You gave me nothin' I Give me the envelope."

"I gave it to you, Whitey," Lambaire almost whimpered. "As soon as you left the room you came back and asked for it."

"Did I come in—quick."

"No, no," the agitation of the big man was pitiable. "You put in your hand and whispered—"

"Amber!" howled the other. He broke with a torrent of curses. "Come on, you fool, he can't have got far."

He flew down the stairs followed by Lambaire. The hall was deserted, the door had been left ajar.

"There he is!"

By the light of a street lamp they saw the fleeing figure and started off in pursuit.

There were few people in sight when a man in his stockinged feet came swiftly from Northumberland Avenue to the Embankment.

"Stop, thief!" bawled Whitey.

The car was further along the Embankment than he had intended it to be, but it was within easy sprinting distance.

"Stop, thief!" shouted Whitey again.

Amber had gained the car when a policeman appeared from nowhere.

"Hold hard," said the man and grasped Amber's arm.

The two pursuers were up to them in an instant.

"That man has stolen something belonging to me," said Whitey, his voice unsteady from his exertions.

"You are entirely mistaken." Amber was more polite and less perturbed than most detected thieves.

"Search him, constable—search him!" roused Whitey.

Amber laughed.

"My dear man, the policeman cannot search me in the street. Haven't you an elementary knowledge of the law?"

A little crowd of night wanderers had collected like magic. More important fact, two other policemen were hurrying towards the group. All this Amber saw and smiled internally, for things had fallen out as he had planned.

"You charge this man," the constable was saying.

"I want my property back," fumed Whitey, "he's a thief: look at him! He's in his stockinged feet! Give me the envelope you stole..."

The two policemen who had arrived elbowed their way through the little crowd, and suddenly Whitey felt sick—ill.

"I agree to go to the station," said Amber smoothly. "I, in turn, accuse these men of burglary."

"Take him off," said Whitey, "my friend and I will follow and charge him."

"We'll take the car," said Amber, "but I insist upon these two men accompanying us."

Here was a situation which Whitey had not foreseen.

They were caught in a trap unless a miracle delivered them.

"We will return to our hotel and get our coats," said Whitey with an air of indifference.

The policeman hesitated, for the request was a reasonable one. "One of you chaps go back with these gentlemen," he said, "and you," to Amber, "had better come along with me. It seems to me I know you."

"I dare say," said Amber as he stepped into the car, "and if those two men get away from your bovine friends you will know me much better than you ever wish to know me."

"None of your lip," said the constable, seating himself by his side.

XX. — CHAPTER THE LAST

"...AND," said the inspector savagely, "if you'd only known the ABC of your duty, constable, you would have brought the two prosecutors here."

Amber was warming himself before the great fire that blazed in the charge- room. A red-faced young policeman was warming himself before the inspector's desk.

"It can't be helped, Inspector," said Amber cheerfully, "I don't know but that if I had been in the constable's place I should have behaved in any other way. Stocking-footed burglar flyin' for his life, eh? Respectable gentlemen toiling in the rear; what would you have done?"

The inspector smiled.

"Well, sir," he admitted, "I think the stockings would have convinced me."

Amber nodded and met the policeman's grateful glance with a grin.

"I don't think there is much use in waiting," said Amber. "Our friends have given the policemen the slip. There is a back entrance to the hotel which I do not doubt they have utilized. Your men could not have the power to make a summary arrest?"

The inspector shook his head.

"The charges are conspiracy and burglary, aren't they?" he asked, "that would require a warrant. A constable could take the responsibility for making a summary arrest, but very few would care to take the risk."

A messenger had brought Amber's shoes and great coat and he was ready to depart.

"I will furnish the yard with the necessary affidavit," he said; "the time has come when we should make a clean sweep. I know almost enough to hang them without the bother of referring to their latest escapade—their complicated frauds extending over years are bad enough; they are distributors, if not actual forgers, of spurious paper money—that's worse from a jury's point of view. Juries understand distributing."

He had sent the car back to Maidstone to bring Sutton. He was not surprised when he came down to breakfast at his hotel to find that not only Frank, but his sister had arrived. Very briefly he told the adventures of the night.

"We will finish with them," he said. "They have ceased to be amusing. A warrant will be issued to-day and with luck we should have them to-night."

* * * * *

Lambaire and Whitey in the meantime had reached the temporary harbour afforded by the Bloomsbury boarding-house where Lambaire lived. Whitey's was ever the master mind in moments of crisis, and now he took charge of the arrangements.

He found a shop in the city that opened early and purchased trunks for the coming journey. Another store supplied him with such of his wardrobe as was replaceable at a moment's notice. He dared not return to his hotel for the baggage he had left.

Lambaire was next to useless. He sat in the sitting-room Whitey had engaged biting his finger nails and cursing helplessly.

"It's no good swearing, Lambaire," said Whitey. "We're up against it—good. We're *peleli*—as the Kaffirs say—finished. Get your cheque-book."

"Couldn't we brazen it out?" querulously demanded the big man, "couldn't we put up a bluff—?"

"Brazen!" sneered Whitey, "you're a cursed fine brazener! You try to brazen a jury! Where's the pass book?"

Reluctantly Lambaire produced it, and Whitey made a brief examination.

"Six thousand three hundred—that's the balance," he said with relish, "and a jolly good balance too. We'll draw all but a hundred. There will be delay if the account is closed."

He took the cheque-book and wrote in his angular caligraphy an order to pay bearer six thousand two hundred pounds. Against the word Director he signed his name and pushed the cheque-book to Lambaire. The other hesitated, then signed.

"Wait a bit," growled Lambaire as his friend reached for the cheque, "who's going to draw this?"

"I am," said Whitey.

Lambaire looked at him suspiciously.

"Why not me?" he asked, "the bank knows me.

"You—you thief! " spluttered Whitey, "you dog! Haven't I trusted you?"

"This is a big matter," said Lambaire doggedly.

With an effort Whitey mastered his wrath.

"Go and change it," he said. "I'm not afraid of you running away—only go quickly—the banks are just opening."

"I don't—I haven't got any suspicion of you, Whitey," said Lambaire with heavy affability, "but business is business."

"Don't jaw—go," said his companion tersely. If the truth be told, Whitey recognized the danger of visiting the bank. There was a possibility that a warrant had already been issued and that the bank would be watched. There was a chance, however, that some delay might occur, and in his old chivalrous way he had been willing to take the risk.

Lambaire went to his room before he departed, and was gone for half an hour. He found Whitey standing with his back to the fire in a meditative mood.

"Here I am, you see." Lambaire's tone was one of gentle raillery. "I haven't run away."

"No," admitted Whitey. "I trust you more than you trust me—though you half made up your mind to bolt with the swag when you came out of the bank." .

Lambaire's face went red.

"How—how do you know—what d'ye mean?" he demanded noisily.

"I followed you," said Whitey simply, "in a taxi-cab."

"Is that what you call trusting me? 11 demanded Lambaire with some bitterness.

"No," said Whitey without shame, "that's what I call takin' reasonable precautions."

Lambaire laughed, an unusual thing for him to do.

He pulled from his breast pockets two thick pads of bank-notes.

"There's your lot, and there's mine," he said, "they are in fifties—I'll count them for you."

Deftly he fingered the notes, turning them rapidly as an accountant turns the leaves of his ledger. There were sixty-two.

Whitey folded them and put them into his pocket.

"Now what's your plan?" asked Whitey.

"The Continent," said Lambaire. "I'll leave by the Harwich route for Holland—we had better separate."

Whitey nodded.

"I'll get out by way of Ireland," he lied. He looked at his watch. It was nearly ten o'clock.

"I shall see you—sometime," he said turning as he left the room, and Lambaire nodded. When he returned the big man had gone.

There is a train which leaves for the Continent at eleven from Victoria—a very dangerous train as Whitey knew, for it is well watched. There was another which left at the same hour from Holborn—this stops at Heme Hill.

Whitey resolved to take a tourist ticket at an office in Ludgate Hill and a taxi-cab to Heme Hill.

He purchased the ticket and was leaving the office, when a thought struck him.

He crossed to the counter where the moneychangers sit. "Let me have a hundred pounds' worth of French money."

He took two fifty-pound notes and pushed them through the grill.

The clerk looked at them, fingered them, then looked at Whitey.

"Notice anything curious about these?" he asked drily.

"No."

There was a horrible sinking sensation in Whitey's heart.

"They are both numbered the same," said the clerk, "and they are forgeries."

Mechanically Whitey took the bundle of notes from his pocket and examined them. They were all of the same number.

His obvious perturbation saved him from an embarrassing inquiry.

"Have you been sold?"

"I have," muttered the duped man. He took the notes the man offered him and walked out.

A passing taxi drew to the kerb at his uplifted hand. He gave the address of Lambaire's lodging.

Lambaire had gone when he arrived: he had probably left before Whitey. Harwich was a blind —Whitey knew that.

He went to Lambaire's room. In his flight Lambaire had left many things behind. Into one of the trunks so left Whitey stuck the bundle of forgeries. If he was to be captured he would not be found in possession of these damning proofs of villainy. A search of the room at first revealed no clue to Lambaire's destination, then Whitey happened upon a tourist's guide. It opened naturally at one page, which meant that one page had been consulted more frequently than any other.

"Winter excursions to the Netherlands, eh?" said Whitey; "that's not a bad move, Lammie: no splits watch excursion trains."

The train left Holborn at a quarter to eleven by way of Queensborough- Flushing. He looked at his watch: it wanted five minutes to the quarter, and to catch that train seemed an impossibility. Then an idea came to him. There was a telephone in the hall of the boarding-house usually well patronized. It was his good luck that he reached it before another boarder came. It was greater luck that he got through to the traffic manager's office at Victoria with little delay.

"I want to know," he asked rapidly, "if the ten forty-five excursion from Holborn stops at any London stations?"

"Every one of 'em," was the prompt reply, "as far as Penge: we pick up all through the suburbs."

"What time is it due away from Penge?"

He waited in a fume of impatience whilst the official consulted a time- table.

"Eleven eighteen," was the reply.

There was time. Just a little over half an hour He fled from the house. No taxi was in sight; but there was a rank at no great distance. He had not gone far, however, before an empty cab overtook him.

"Penge Station," he said. "I'll give you a sovereign over your fare if you get there within half an hour."

The chauffeur's face expressed his doubt.

"I'll try," he said.

Through London that day a taxi-cab moved at a rate which was considerably in excess of the speed limit. Clear of the crowded West End, the road was unhampered by traffic to any great extent, but it was seventeen minutes past eleven when the cab pulled up before Penge Station.

The train was already at the platform and Whitey went up the stairs two at a time.

"Ticket," demanded the collector.

"I've no ticket—I'll pay on the train."

"You can't come on without a ticket, sir," said the man.

The train was within a few feet of him and was slowly moving, and Whitey made a dart, but a strong hand grasped him and pushed him back and the gate clanged in his face.

He stood leaning against the wall, his face white, his fingers working convulsively.

Something in his appearance moved the collector.

"Can't be helped, sir," he said. "I had—"

He stopped and looked in the direction of the departing train.

Swiftly he leant down and unlocked the door.

"Here—quick," he said, "she's stopped outside the station—there's a signal against her. You'll just catch it."

The rear carriages were not clear of the platform and Whitey, sprinting along, scrambled into the guard's van just as the train was moving off again.

He sank down into the guard's seat. Whitey was a man of considerable vitality. Ordinarily the exertion he had made would not have inconvenienced him, but now he was suffering from something more than physical distress.

"On me!" he muttered again and again," to put them on me!"

It was not the loss of the money that hurt him, it was not Lambaire's treachery—he knew Lambaire through and through. It was the substitution of the notes and the terrible risk his estimable friend had inflicted on him.

In his cold way Whitey had decided. He had a code of his own. Against Amber he had no grudge. Such spaces of thought as he allowed him were of a complimentary character. He recognized the master mind, paid tribute to the shrewdness of the man who had beaten him at his own game.

Nor against the law which pursued him—for instinct told him that there would be no mercy from Amber now.

It was against Lambaire that his rage was directed. Lambaire, whose right- hand man he had been in a score of nefarious schemes. They had

been together in bogus companies; they had dealt largely in "Spanish silver"; they had been concerned in most generous systems of forgery. The very notes that Lambaire had employed to fool him with were part of an old stock.

The maker had committed the blunder of giving all the notes the same number.

"They weren't good enough for the public—but good enough for me," thought Whitey, and set his jaw.

The guard tried to make conversation, but his passenger had nothing to say, save " yes " or " no."

It was raining heavily when the train drew up at Chatham, and Whitey with his coat collar turned up, his hat pulled over his eyes and a handkerchief to his mouth, left the guard's van and walked quickly along the train.

The third-class carriages were sparsely filled. It seemed that the " winter excursion " was poorly patronized.

Whitey gave little attention to the thirds— he had an eye for the first-class carriages which were in the main empty. He found his man n the centre of the train—alone. He took him in with a glance of his eye and walked on. The whistle sounded and as the train begun to glide from the platform he turned, opened the door of the carriage and stepped in.

* * * * *

There were other people who knew Lambaire was on the train. Amber came through Kent as fast as a 90 horse power car could carry him. He might have caught the train at Penge had he but known. It would have been better for two people if he had.

With him was a placid inspector from Scotland Yard—by name Fells.

"We shall just do it, I think," said Amber looking at his watch," and anyway you will have people waiting?"

The inspector nodded. Speaking was an effort at the pace the car was travelling.

He roused himself to the extent of expressing his surprise that Amber had troubled to take the journey.

But Amber, who had seen the beginning of the adventure, was no man to hear the end from another. He was out to finish the business, or to see the finish. They reached the quay station as the excursion train came in and hurried along the slippery quay, Already the passengers were beginning their embarkation. By each gangway stood two men watching.

The last passenger was aboard.

"They could not have come," said Amber disappointedly. "If—"

At that moment a railway official came running toward them.

"You gentlemen connected with the police?" he asked, "there's something rum in one of these carriages..." he led the way giving information incoherently, "... gentleman won't get out."

They reached the carriage and Amber it was who opened the door...

"Come along, Whitey," he said quietly.

But the man who sat in one corner of the carriage slowly counting two thick packages of bank-notes took no notice.

"That's a good 'un," he muttered, "an' that's a good 'un—eh, Lammie? These are good—but the other lot was bad. What a fool—fool—fool I Oh, my God, what a fool you always was !"

He groaned the words, swaying from side to side as if in pain.

"Come out," said Amber sharply.

Whitey saw him and rose from his seat.

"Hullo, Amber," he said and smiled, "I'm coming... what about our River of Stars, eh? Here's a pretty business—here's money—look."

He thrust out a handful of notes and Amber started back, for they were splotched and blotted with blood.

"These are good 'uns," said Whitey. His lips were trembling, and in his colourless eyes there was a light which no man had ever seen. "The others were bad 'uns. I had to kill old Lammie—he annoyed me."

And he laughed horribly.

Under the seat they found Lambaire, shot through the heart.

Printed in Great Britain
by Amazon